HURRICANE HEAT

orca sports

HURRICANE HEAT

STEVEN BARWIN

ORCA BOOK PUBLISHERS

Library and Archives Canada Cataloguing in Publication

Barwin, Steven
Hurricane heat / Steven Barwin.
(Orca sports)

Issued also in electronic formats.
ISBN 978-1-4598-0213-1

I. Title. II. Series: Orca sports
PS8553.A7836H87 2013   jc813'.54   C2012-907469-1

First published in the United States, 2013
Library of Congress Control Number: 2012952951

Summary: Years after Travis's parents die in a car crash and he and his younger
sister, Amanda, are separated, Travis sets out to search for her at the risk of losing
an opportunity for a future baseball career.

MIX
Paper from
responsible sources
FSC® C016245
www.fsc.org

*Orca Book Publishers is dedicated to preserving the environment and has printed
this book on Forest Stewardship Council® certified paper.*

Orca Book Publishers gratefully acknowledges the support for its publishing
programs provided by the following agencies: the Government of Canada through
the Canada Book Fund and the Canada Council for the Arts, and the Province of
British Columbia through the BC Arts Council and
the Book Publishing Tax Credit.

Cover photography by Corbis
Author photo by Jenna Grossi

ORCA BOOK PUBLISHERS
PO Box 5626, Stn. B
Victoria, BC Canada
V8R 6S4

ORCA BOOK PUBLISHERS
PO Box 468
Custer, WA USA
98240-0468

www.orcabook.com
Printed and bound in Canada.

16 15 14 13 • 4 3 2 1

To my grandmother, Ettie Nochomovitz,
who taught me almost everything I know
about baseball. You are greatly missed.

chapter one

I watched the baseball swerve below the batter's powerful swing and punch into the catcher's glove with a loud thump. The score was tied 5-5 at the bottom of the seventh inning. I wiped the sweat from my forehead. It felt great to be distracted by a heated game.

The batter spat onto the ground. He was a right-handed hitter. Even though I didn't know his name, batting history or anything else, with two balls and no strikes

I knew the pitcher had to go with a fastball down low on the batter's right side. Attack his weak spot, where he couldn't swing the bat around fast enough to make contact. The pitcher wound up and released the ball. It started up high and then broke, falling down and to the right. I shook my head. He might as well have fed the batter the baseball on a silver tray. It arrived in the bottom left side of the batter's box. The batter stepped into the pitch and made contact, with a loud crack. I watched the ball rip through the air and land deep in right field. The go-ahead run made it safely to third base with a triple.

Someone in the stands said, "Let's go! You can do it!"

The next batter took a few practice swings and stepped to the plate. The pitch crossed the plate too high, but the batter swung, nerves probably getting the better of him. The foul ball popped up high in my direction. I had it in my crosshairs and watched it reach the top of its arc and begin a fast descent. In the row ahead of me, a young girl no more than ten years old shrieked and buried her head under her mother's arm.

I stretched out my bare hand and felt the ball wallop into it, just above the little girl and her mother.

The mother looked at me for a moment, her eyes wide. "Thank you."

She and her daughter weren't the only ones in the crowd surprised by my catch. People started to clap. I smiled, half embarrassed, handed the ball to the girl and made my way out of the stands.

I crossed the parking lot and headed toward the high school. That's where I was going before the game lured me over. I needed to stay on task, keep moving. My palm still stung. When I looked at it, it was red, but I could move my fingers.

I got to the front of the school and tried the doors. They were all locked. Banging on them didn't work either.

At the side of the school, I found a scratched-up metal door. I knocked on it with my shoe. To my surprise, it jarred opened.

A large unshaven janitor appeared, wearing blue uniform pants and a matching button-down with the sleeves rolled up. He had a suspicious look on his face. "Yeah?"

"I'm looking for a girl," I said.

He smiled and moved to close the door.

I wedged my foot in the doorway. After all the people I'd approached, questioned and bugged in the last two weeks, "I'm looking for a girl" wasn't my best opening line. "Her name's Amanda, and she's my sister," I added. "I think she goes to this school."

"Sorry."

"People used to say we look alike. She's got the same black hair as me, but obviously hers isn't buzz-cut. There's Hispanic blood on my mom's side, so she's a little dark like me."

He caught a glimpse of my watch. It was gold with a steel band and black face. I figured he was probably wondering what a teenager in a hoodie was doing walking around with a gold watch. He didn't know that it was my dad's watch. It was vintage, and the only thing of his I got after the accident.

The caretaker shrugged his shoulders. "Exams ended today. No one around but me."

"Is there any way I can take a look inside?"

"What for?"

"I might see her picture on the wall or something. She was into sports. I'd guess on the swimming team." I knew it was a long shot.

"Sorry, kid. Wish I could help you, but I can't."

I was frustrated. I had come to California to find Amanda. My younger sister. Five years ago, our parents died in a car accident. I was only eleven and she was nine. We didn't exactly get along back then. The social worker tried to find someone to take both of us, but he couldn't. Amanda went to one foster home, and I went to another. When her foster family announced one day that they were moving to California, that was it for Amanda and me. I never heard from or saw her again.

Five months ago, I found a postcard sitting on top of a pile of mail in the kitchen. The postcard had a picture of the Hermosa Beach Pier on the front and my name on the back. I knew it was from her because Amanda was in California. But I still didn't know exactly where, because except for my name and address, the postcard was blank.

When summer holidays arrived, I convinced my foster parents to allow me to go look for her. They were nice enough to drive me the six and a half hours to Hermosa and set me up in a room at a family friend's house. They even helped me get a job as a dishwasher. I'd do anything to find Amanda. She's my only real family. Blood. That's gotta be worth something. And maybe, just maybe, she will feel the same.

A loud cheer erupted from the base-ball diamond. When I rounded the school, the field had almost emptied. By the time I reached the parking lot, there was nobody left in the stands. I considered taking a shortcut home across the field. But I hadn't stepped on a baseball diamond in a long time.

I must've looked funny just standing in front of the empty field staring at it. I stepped across the first-base foul line and entered the diamond. I thought about my last baseball game, five years ago. I knelt down and brushed the perfectly manicured grass with my fingers.

The unmistakable shape of a baseball caught my eye. It was lodged under the home bench. I walked over, picked it up and dusted it off against my shorts. When I centered myself on the pitching mound, I could still feel the tenderness in my palm from catching the foul ball barehanded.

The last game I ever played was in Phoenix. I had been in a neighborhood league. My coach told me baseball would take me far in life. He said dreaming about major-league baseball was not dreaming too big. I pictured myself in that last game, holding the runner on third to make sure he stayed put. Beyond him, the tip of Camelback Mountain stretched up in the distance—it actually looked like a camel's hump. I turned my attention back on the batter and wondered where my parents were. They came to all my games. Their absence distracted me enough to hang one over the plate and not only lose the inning but also the game...

I still missed baseball, after all these years.

I placed my index and middle fingers across the ball's seams. My thumb rested on the white leather. Lifting the ball over my shoulder, I whipped it angrily at the plate. It smashed into the backstop, and I realized two things. First, I still had a really good pitch. Second, there was a guy watching me. And clapping.

chapter two

"Nice pitch. Where do you play?" he asked. The guy wore a number eleven jersey with Hermosa Hurricanes written across the front. "My name's Ethan."

"Travis," I said.

He had a windblown look, blond hair jutting in every direction. His bangs ran down to a straight edge stopping just above his eyes, framing his black Wayfarer sunglasses.

"Is that your ball?" I was about to get it for him, but he stopped me, saying he'd just come back for his sunglasses.

"You're the guy who caught that fly ball in the stands with one hand."

I nodded and held out my palm, half expecting it to still be red. He asked again where I played. When I told him I didn't play anywhere, he gave me a puzzled look.

"I'm a catcher with the Hurricanes. We're an eighteen-and-under select team. I've worked with a lot of pitchers, and you have a great arm."

I smiled. It had been a long time since I had thrown, and I'd wondered if I still had the touch.

"I'd like to see it up close. Want to throw me one?"

I shrugged my shoulders. Just one pitch, I told myself. I stepped on the mound while Ethan retrieved the ball. He grabbed his catcher's glove from his bag, tossed me the ball and squatted behind the plate. My fingers rolled the ball in my hand, and I decided to throw a fastball.

I stood at a slight angle, one foot on the rubber and the ball in my hand, chest high. I started my windup, extending the baseball behind me with my left hand. I felt how rusty I really was. I released the ball, and it smacked into Ethan's glove.

"Wow, I felt that through my glove!" He approached me. "Do you live in Hermosa?"

"Sort of."

"You should try out for the team."

"I don't really have a lot of time for baseball."

"But you've played before. I can tell."

I nodded.

Ethan spent the next seven minutes trying to sell me. He told me about the league and some of the tournaments. He also mentioned that scouts were always coming by, looking to hand out college scholarships.

"But your season's already started," I said.

"Our roster isn't frozen. Come out, show the coach what you have, and you'll make the team. Trust me."

I fantasized for a moment about getting a scholarship so I could quit my dishwashing job and go to college. I let my mind wander to getting picked up by a major-league team. Then I thought about Amanda, and it all vanished. I needed to find her first. "I'll think about it."

Dirty dishes overflowed the sink when I arrived at work the next day. Washing pots and pans in the back of a taco restaurant wasn't exactly my dream summer job. Hola Tacos was a low-key, no-thrills, notch-above-a-dive kind of restaurant, but the food was good, and it was always busy. I used a tap hose to spray and scrub down plates and cups before they went into a dishwasher. No matter how many I cleaned, the pile never seemed to go down. It was no wonder my boss called the area where I worked the dish pit. The important thing was, I had a job. And it came with one big plus. Jessie. She was a waitress who didn't often get to the deep bowels of the kitchen where I spent my shift. But I had a clean sight of her when she picked up her food orders. She had bleached blond hair almost always tied in two braids and was pretty enough to not have to wear makeup. My interest in her wasn't just physical. I knew there was a lot more to her behind those turquoise eyes.

After the lunch rush, I noticed her reaching to untie her apron. So I asked my boss if I could take my fifteen minutes. He wanted to know if all the plates were clean, and I tried not to laugh. All the plates would never be clean—it was a never-ending pile—but I nodded, and he let me go.

I darted out the back, crossed Pier Avenue and headed toward the Hermosa Beach Pier. I approached my favorite—well, Jessie's favorite—smoothie shop, the Pineapple Hut. She was already on the patio, in black Lululemon pants and a white T-shirt, talking on her cell and sipping a smoothie. I got a drink and found a table outside. The afternoon was balmy, and seagulls circled overhead. I pulled out the postcard and placed it on the table. I stared at it and thought about what Ethan had said.

It had been a long time since I had played baseball, but I couldn't stop thinking about it. A college scholarship would have made my parents proud. My dad had wanted me to ride baseball all the way to the majors. This could be a new beginning.

"How's it going?"

It took me a moment to realize Jessie was talking to me. I never expected to have a conversation with her. I smiled awkwardly.

"What you looking at?" she asked.

I covered the postcard with both hands.

"Sorry," she said.

"No, it's okay. Just a long story." But I didn't want my conversation with her to dry up. "You from around here?" I asked.

"Yup."

"You been working at Hola Tacos long?"

"Just summers. I work so I can surf. Now you know everything about me, and I know nothing about you."

"Oh."

She laughed. "It was a joke."

I laughed, even though the joke had passed. I told her I had just moved to

Hermosa from Phoenix, leaving out the complicated stuff about my family.

"I've been there. It's a great city." She played with a silver medallion hanging from her neck. "That part of your long story?"

I didn't know how to respond. "Want to hear it?"

She smiled. "Is our break long enough?"

This time I laughed on cue.

Jessie picked up her drink and took a seat at my table.

"I'm out here looking for my sister." I held out the postcard. "She sent this, and I think it's a clue."

Jessie examined the picture of Hermosa pier on the front and then flipped it over. "Except for your name, it's blank."

I nodded. "This is all I have to go on."

"How old is she?"

"Fourteen."

"My sister's the same age. I think she knew an Amanda."

I looked at Jessie and thought, *There are a lot of Amandas out there.*

"I'll ask her," Jessie said. "What's your cell?"

I took a deep breath. Not only did I have a lead on an Amanda, but Jessie would now have my cell number.

chapter three

Anxious about my first game, I wasn't able to sleep the last two nights. When I arrived the Saturday morning, pregame warm-up was in session. Hurricanes players did laps around the outfield. I spotted the back of Ethan's jersey, number eleven. When he saw me, he waved me over. I slipped in behind him and jogged with the team.

"Glad you showed," Ethan said between breaths.

I nodded and tried to keep up. I knew the other players were wondering who the new guy was. This field wasn't as groomed as the one by the high school. At the 375 marker in center field, homes of all shapes and sizes filled the horizon. While one home looked like a college bunker, another had white stucco, large windows, balconies in the front and back and a rooftop terrace that must've had a perfect view of the Pacific.

"I have this for you." Ethan handed me a folded-up piece of paper. "For later."

I slipped it into my pocket.

The coach waved everyone in to grab their gloves.

"That's Coach Robert," said Ethan.

I nodded.

"Quick practice for the pitchers," the coach said.

Ethan motioned me over. "Follow me."

While the infielders threw the ball around the bases and the outfielders practiced throwing long balls, a pitcher tossed the ball to Ethan behind home plate. I stood next to another pitcher, number seven, just off the mound. He didn't take any notice of me, and I didn't feel like starting small talk. He eventually stepped onto the mound to throw some pitches. Behind him, I noticed the other team starting to arrive. Then I felt a tap on my shoulder. It was Coach Robert. He smelled like coconut suntan lotion. His hair was speckled grey and cropped almost military style under his hat. He wasn't tall, but the muscles defining his jersey told me he was tough.

Coach Robert asked us to switch again. Number seven placed the ball firmly in my glove—a glove I had bought the day before at an outlet store. Bleachers rose in seven levels behind home plate. At the top of the bleachers, two announcers prepped for the game in a small green wooden hut with a rolled-up window. I released the ball from my left hand with a lot of power, and it found the strike zone.

"Hold on," was all Coach Robert said to me. He called for a player named Wilson, who grabbed a bat and stood in front of Ethan.

I waited, giving him a couple of rehearsal swings, and then released the same pitch. Wilson went down swinging.

The coach from the other team approached. "Hey, Robert, if you're gonna pass, we'll take him!"

"Thanks for the offer, but no thanks, Paul." Coach Robert guided me toward the Hurricanes bench as the Surf City Buckeyes started their warm-up. He held out a jersey. "Job's yours, if you want it."

"Okay," I said.

"Good answer. I need a closer. Get the waiver signed, and make the payment before next Tuesday's game. Welcome to the Hurricanes."

Ethan was the first and only player to welcome me to the team.

Tuesday morning I arrived at the bench dressed in my Hurricanes uniform. Coach Robert was in the middle of a pep talk. "In addition to league games, our ball club will be competing in some high-level tournaments.

But for now, we have a game to win. Let's start this season off with a win today."

An hour and a half later, I was still sitting on the edge of the bench in the same spot as when the game started. In front of me, I had the paper Ethan had given me at the last game. It was a cheat sheet for catcher-to-pitcher call signals. When I wasn't watching the game, I tried to memorize them.

With us leading 6 to 5 in the bottom of the seventh and last inning, the Buckeyes had a runner on third and two outs. Coach Robert dashed onto the field to talk to the pitcher with Ethan. The coach looked over at the bench and tapped his left hand. That was his silent call for me. I grabbed my glove and trotted to the mound.

Coach adjusted his baseball hat. "Tying run's on third, and the go-ahead's up to bat. He's a lefty, so take him outside."

I nodded. As a left-handed pitcher, I had the advantage over a lefty hitter, especially if I could place a breaking ball down and away from him.

Coach dropped the baseball in my glove. The batter kept his distance while I took a couple of warm-up pitches. Alone on the mound, I stared at the baseball until the umpire called, "Game on." The batter stepped into the box. It was crunch time. Ethan showed one finger. It was the signal for a curveball. He then showed four fingers, which meant he wanted the pitch to break away from the batter.

I placed my middle finger along the bottom seam of the ball and my thumb on the back seam. I released the ball. It started high toward the outside of the strike zone and kept on going. The pitch ran wide and dinged off the fence. I ran to cover home base as Ethan hustled to retrieve the ball. But the runner on third stayed put.

Back on the mound, I tried to put the embarrassing moment out of my mind. Ethan flipped the same sign and same location. I pitched, trying to follow his directions. The ball started nice and high, and it began to drop as if on cue. Problem was, it didn't stop dropping. It pummeled into the dirt, and Ethan struggled to contain it. Two and oh, and I was in trouble.

Ethan lifted his mask and approached me on the mound. "You okay?"

I didn't respond, thinking the answer was obvious.

"It's just me and you out here. Block everything else out." He covered his mouth with his glove. "What do you want to throw?"

I did the same with my glove. "Fastball."

He nodded and went back to his place behind home plate.

With two fingers on the seams of the baseball, I released it, catching the batter off guard.

The umpire yelled, "Strike!"

Relief. I sent another toward the batter. He swung for the ball, but it broke away and down. The count was two and two.

Ethan tossed the ball back with a big smile. He exchanged a few signals with the coach, and then he asked for a fastball, inside but center. I checked the runner on third before starting the pitch. The fastball sped out of my hand, and the batter leaned into the pitch. He swung hard, and I think he was as surprised as me to see the ball in Ethan's glove.

The Hurricanes swarmed off the bench and surrounded me. Somewhere in the celebration huddle, Ethan found me. Coach Robert had to remind us to shake hands with the other team. After a long procession of high-fives and good-game handshakes with the Buckeyes, I reached our bench and heard my cell phone ring.

I picked it up. "Hello?"

"Travis, it's me."

"Jessie?"

"I think I found your sister. Meet me at the Pineapple Hut in ten minutes."

chapter four

My baseball cleats clicked across the street to the Pineapple Hut. I found Jessie with a supersized smoothie.

She unraveled her straw from its wrapper with her teeth and plunged it into her drink. "I didn't know you played baseball."

"I was kind of talked into it."

"Okay. So I was telling my sister about you, and she said she knew an Amanda in her class, but they weren't friends or anything. Then I thought of this." She unzipped her backpack, then stopped and offered a disclaimer, the way a lawyer would. "If this isn't her, I'm really sorry."

"It's okay."

She handed me the yearbook. "It's from last year."

I noticed a dog-eared page and went right to it. Scrolling through the sea of faces, I searched for Amanda. I paused at a girl with dark-brown hair, outnumbered by all the blonds, but it wasn't her. Then another dark-haired girl caught my attention. When I saw her eyes, I didn't have to check the name to know it was Amanda.

"Is that her?"

I had forgotten that Jessie was across from me. "Yes."

"Oh my god, you found her! Aren't you stoked?"

I was overwhelmed. In the photo, Amanda looked amazing. Happy. I thanked Jessie over and over again, and then she pointed at the name. Amanda Miller.

I hadn't even noticed. She must have been adopted and changed her name.

A loud voice interrupted us. "There you are!"

I looked up to see Ethan, dressed in uniform.

"What's going on?" There was a notice-able edge to his voice. "Everyone on the team is wondering if you quit."

"Something important came up," I said.

Ethan eyed Jessie. "I can see."

"No, not her—"

"Then what?"

I forced him to sit down and told him about my search for Amanda.

"You're an idiot," he said.

Jessie responded before I could. "Excuse me?"

Ethan smiled. "You should have said something. I think I can help."

With the Jeep's roof off, the battering wind filled Ethan's white Wrangler. In the back,

Jessie's hair thrashed madly in every direction. The blue of the Pacific seemed even more mesmerizing as I rode along the highway with Jessie and Ethan.

Jessie asked how long we'd known each other.

Ethan looked at her through the rear-view mirror. "A couple of weeks."

"And you got him on the baseball team?"

"I really didn't give him an option to refuse. You have to see this guy pitch. He's incredible."

"He's exaggerating," I said.

Ethan turned to me. "You kidding me? I had to ice my hand after this morning's game!"

I looked back at Jessie. "See what I mean?"

"Maybe I need to come and see this for myself."

"Any time," Ethan said.

"So, Travis, were you adopted, like your sister?" Jessie asked.

An image popped into my brain of an eleven-year-old me sitting at the dinner table, head so low it was almost swimming in my cereal. It wasn't that I didn't like my foster parents, the Wilsons. It was just that they weren't my real parents. They were nice people who cared about me and were doing the state of Arizona a favor until I turned eighteen. "No, I was never adopted."

Ethan pulled the Jeep into a one-story strip plaza painted bright yellow. I scanned the stores and didn't see anything that stood out. He pulled into a parking spot, and we all got out.

Ethan leaned against his Jeep. "In the corner, there's a foster family agency."

I asked him how he knew about this place, and he pointed to a Korean barbecue restaurant next door and said it was the best around.

Memories of Amanda invaded my thoughts as I took a step toward the agency. After Amanda and I were separated, a woman at the foster family agency in Phoenix had gotten Amanda and me together for visits in a place like this. The agency had tried hard to keep a relationship between us going, so I could never figure out why they had let Amanda move to California.

"Hey, Jess. I know the answer to finding my sister might be through those doors, but I can't go in."

chapter five

Jessie opened the door to the agency and tapped me on my back. It felt less like a nudge and more like a push. I had to try and get contact information on Amanda. A woman with half-rimmed glasses and a polka-dot shirt greeted us from behind a desk. She looked up from her computer and offered a half smile, as if distrust was already brewing. Jessie gave me another push, strong enough to launch me forward.

"My name's Travis. I was wondering...if I needed to..." I didn't know what to say or how to say it.

"He's trying to find his sister," Jessie said.

The woman picked up the phone.

Was she ignoring me?

After a few whispered exchanges followed by some uh-huhs, she directed us to have a seat. I took it as a good sign.

Jessie turned to me. "I feel like I'm waiting to see the doctor."

"More like the dentist," I said.

Eventually, the receptionist led us through a doorway. There were some offices and a carpeted area with books and toys and a mural of a boy reading a book under a tree on a grassy field. Part of the tree was cut off by light switches. The carpeted area was the kind of space my visits with Amanda had been held in.

An office door opened, and Jessie and I were sat in front of a tall woman in a green suit.

"My name's Beverly. How can I help you?"

"My name is Travis Barkley. My younger sister is Amanda Miller. We're from Phoenix and were put in different foster families. Amanda's family adopted her, and they moved out here. I'm trying to find her."

"And you are?"

"Jessie. Friend."

"As much as I'd like to help you, I can't."

"Why not?" I asked.

"I'm not legally allowed to give out information on a minor."

"I really need to find her," I said. "Is there any—"

"Plus, I can't give out information on a minor without permission from the adoptive family."

"So I have to get permission from the people I can't find?" I asked.

"I'm sorry," said Beverly.

I shook my head. Beverly wished me good luck on my journey, which meant, "time to go." I followed Jessie out, but it didn't feel right to be giving up that easily. If Beverly could help in any way at all, no matter how small, it would be worth it.

I let Jessie get a few strides ahead, then spun around and caught Beverly off guard. "There has to be something you can do to help me find Amanda."

"Sorry, but you need to leave," said Beverly.

"I can't give up."

"It's not about giving up," Beverly said. "It's about working within the system like everyone else."

"Please. I'm begging you to help me."

"Look, part of your problem is that you're a minor. To access information about your sister, you need to be eighteen. The age of majority."

chapter six

There were three of us in the car, but from the silence, you wouldn't have known it. I was deflated. Amanda was out there somewhere. It was getting harder to believe that I was going to locate her. I didn't want to feel down on myself, but it was clear the odds were not in my favor.

Ethan broke the silence. "I feel horrible."

"It's not your fault," I said.

"That lady could've helped us," Jessie said.

I shifted lower in my seat to avoid the blinding sun. "No, she was just doing her job. Everyone's just been trying to do their job the entire time I've been living with the Wilsons. As Beverly said, you can't blame anyone—it's the system."

"But the system," Jessie said, "is the people."

I didn't have an answer for her. For the first time since coming to the west coast, I wondered if my foster parents were right. They had never *said* I shouldn't search for Amanda. It was more the looks they shared when we talked about it. It was as if they thought I was chasing a ghost. Each day of the summer that slipped away was one less day to find Amanda and one more day toward returning to my last year of high school empty-handed.

Ethan made a right turn out of the traffic. "So, I screwed up that time. You have to let me make it up to you. I know a great place for dinner."

I nodded.

"You in, Jessie?" Ethan said to her.

"If you're buying" she said.

"Sure, why not?"

She smiled. "I'm in."

We pulled up to a place called the Deep Fryer. It was a red shack with white paneling and was no bigger than a trailer-park home. A colorful canopy with the words *Great American Food* stretched over two slider windows. A blue, red and white World Series-style pennant hung from the counter.

Ethan assured Jessie and me that the Deep Fryer served the best cheeseburgers around.

"Manny," Ethan said, "these are my friends, Jessie and Travis."

Manny, who looked forty-five and Hispanic, smiled at us and said, "You have got a good friend here."

"Yes, and he's paying too," Jessie said.

Manny laughed. "See what I mean?"

"So, Manny, how are your milkshakes?" Jessie asked.

"Best in town."

"I'll take one." She looked at me. "Make that two."

37

Ethan rolled his eyes and reached for his wallet.

Manny busied himself over the grill. "You guys going to the cages too?"

"Cages?" Jessie asked.

"Batting cages. They're in the back," said Ethan.

"You know," Jessie said, "I'm more of a surf and yoga girl. But—"

"Let me guess," Ethan said. "Because I'm paying, you'd like to try it."

She aimed at him as if her fingers were a gun and pulled the trigger.

When the burgers came out, they were the size of my face. Now I understood why Ethan loved this place. The onion rings were so big, I could have worn them around my wrists. After doing some serious damage to our burgers, Ethan and I watched Jessie losing the battle to hers.

Ethan handed Jessie and me a couple of tokens, and we each took a bat. It was obvious when we got to the cages that

Manny loved baseball. The batting cages were in excellent condition. I found a Louisville that was the right weight—a little heavy. Then I entered a cage with Jessie and Ethan to my right. At the far end of the cage, a pitching machine was aimed at me, a long line of baseballs ready to be launched. Jessie asked if we were ready. I inserted my token and took my position in the bright blue rectangular box to the right of home plate. I heard my machine sputter to life, and I braced myself for the first pitch. It had been a long time since I had been to a cage. The machine lobbed its first yellow ball toward me. I swung and missed. I made sure to connect with the next one, pelting it high into the meshed ceiling. It dropped to the ground and slowly rolled down a short incline and into a hole in the cement floor. The sound of a perfect ping echoed from Ethan's cage, and I looked over. "Nice one."

"Thanks. I got that one in the sweet spot."

I prepped for my next pitch and sent it in the same direction as before. Maybe I was too frustrated tonight to really get behind the ball. Jessie let out a small scream as she missed her ball. I swung with everything I had on my next pitch, batting a line drive toward my pitching machine that almost went back inside. "Did you see that? Almost got a hole in one!"

After finishing our sets, the three of us gathered behind the cages.

"Jessie, what you have to do is bend your knees and get behind the ball." Ethan demonstrated with his bat.

I jumped in. "Yeah, but you also have to keep your head up and not swing too early."

Jessie stepped back. "Guys. I just missed a couple. I'm not that bad, considering I'm not pros like you."

Ethan shrugged. "Hey, I was just trying to help out."

"So, then, why don't we make the next round a little more fun?" Jessie smiled.

"You talking about a competition?" I asked.

"I'm in," Ethan said. "What does the winner get?"

"I don't know. How about, it's not what the winner gets, but what the loser has to do," I said.

"Done!" Ethan said. "Whatever it is, we're talking clothes off, right?"

Jessie laughed. "Then how about the loser becomes target practice?"

"Okay," said Ethan, "but I'm now wishing I never brought it up."

"How about just bragging rights?" I said.

"Deal," Jessie said. "Two out of three means Ethan's outvoted."

Ethan sighed. "Whatever. Let's just set up the rules and do it."

Jessie smiled at me. We couldn't believe how competitive he was.

He pointed. "There are numbers, one to four, along the sides. You hit it, you get the point. The ground and up high are zero."

I returned to my cage. If I had totaled my last round, I probably wouldn't have had more than ten points. With the tokens in and the first ball heading my way, Ethan yelled out, "Four," and I missed my ball. Ethan smiled. If he wanted to play that kind of game, I had to up mine. With the next pitch, I loosened my grip and stepped into the ball. I yelled out "Three" at the same time as Jessie. The next five pitches moved my score up to eighteen. I would have to hit my fours to beat Ethan. Whether I won or lost, at least my mind was off Amanda for a while.

"It's gonna be close," Ethan said.

Jessie said, "And no cheating."

Ethan fired back with, "Only losers have to cheat."

"Oh, this is so on!" Jessie said.

I tried to focus on my own game. *No offense, Jessie, but I don't want to lose to you.* The baseball approached. I lined my bat up down low to get a small amount of height on the ball, and then my cell phone went off in the front pocket of my jeans. First a vibration, then a full-on ring. I rarely got calls, so I was curious enough to take it. I stepped away from the pitch, rested the bat against the cage and answered the call. "Hello?"

"Travis. Hi, dear."

It was Tracy, my foster mom.

"Oh, hi." Another ball zipped past. "Everything okay?" I asked.

"Yes, of course. I wanted to let you know that I signed your baseball waiver and emailed it to the league yesterday."

Another ball whizzed over the plate. "Thank you." I reached for my bat.

"So you picked up baseball?"

I tried not to sound like I was rushing her off the phone, but I was. "Yes."

"I think that's just wonderful. And how is it going with your search?"

Yet another ball shot past. I was losing my opportunity to catch up to Ethan. "I've hit speed bumps. But I haven't given up."

"That's great to hear. Glad that you're okay. I don't want to take up more of your minutes. I'll call you later at the house, and you can fill me in on work and the team. John says hi. Take care."

"Thanks." I hung up and stepped into the box, missing another opportunity.

Steven Barwin

Ethan said, "Too bad about the distraction."

"Don't let him get to you, Travis," said Jessie.

"He's not. I want a rematch." I swung, and the ball hit within the four zone. I yelled it out extra loudly.

"There are no rematches. Just take the defeat," said Ethan.

Before the next pitch, I looked over to Jessie. "Tell me you're doing well."

"Is twenty-six good?"

"You have twenty-six?" Ethan said.

"I'm guessing that means I'm doing well," she said.

"Yes," I said. "Keep it up, Jessie."

I knew there couldn't have been more than two baseballs left. I made contact, and the ball flew in a perfect line toward the pitching machine. It looked like it was going to hit it, and then the baseball disappeared. "Did you see that?"

Jessie's and Ethan's machines stopped, and they approached.

"What're your totals?" Ethan asked.

Maybe they hadn't heard me. "Did you see my last shot? I think I might have got it back in the machine."

"Impossible," Ethan said.

I crossed the yellow do-not-cross markings and walked toward my machine. Ethan and Jessie followed. "How many points would I get for that?"

"Like, a hundred," Jessie said.

I raised my hands in celebration. The ball was lodged in the pitching machine. "What are the chances!"

Jessie gave me a high five and announced that I had won before Ethan could even protest.

chapter seven

So far there had been two eras in my life. One was AD, the era after the death of my parents—the one I was living in now. The other was BD, the time before the death of my parents. In the BD era, life was good. I played ball all the time. In fact, things seemed simpler then, like the pitching philosophy of one of my favorite coaches, Coach Jacobs. He said, *Pitching's simple— just keep the ball away from the bat.*

I wasn't sure if it was a metaphor for life, but I chuckled every time I thought about it.

Unfortunately, our team wasn't following his advice on Thursday. The Royals were enjoying a three-run lead in the third inning, and I was getting restless. Feeling like the odd man out, I was at the very end of the bench, sitting so close to the edge that there was barely enough room for both cheeks. Two other pitchers sat beside me, in conversation. When they laughed, I wasn't entirely convinced they weren't laughing at me. They had matching sundrenched-blond hair, dark suntans and whiter-than-white teeth. I wasn't exactly good at small talk, and they didn't attempt to engage me. I was the new guy, and they were doing a great job of making me feel that way. I figured they didn't even know my name. What did it matter? At the end of the summer, I'd be heading home and would never see them again. So I tried not to let their chitchat get to me.

Coach Robert paced in a small rectangular pattern. He broke from it when one of our guys flied out and ended our turn at bat. I felt the bench rise as it cleared of players, and then it was just the two pitchers and me. I moved to a more comfortable spot.

One of the pitchers stopped me. "You can't move."

The other one chirped up. "Yeah, this is our pitching order. You're at the end of the line."

I returned to my spot. "I didn't know."

They continued their conversation, and I tried to focus on the game. Another tip my old coach had given me was that some of the highest-paid pitchers spend most of their time warming the bench. The smart ones keep their minds in the game, studying the batters. I was a bit intimidated to be playing again. I needed to find a flaw in a player's stance or swing to get reconnected. A batter who stood too close to the plate was my favorite. I could get inside, send him a message and take control of the situation.

"Mr. T!"

It was Coach Robert yelling, and it took me a second to realize that I was Mr. T. I sat up. "Yes."

"You're going in," he said.

"I am?"

"Is there an echo? Do you have a problem with that? 'Cause I can get—"

"No. I'm good to go."

"That's the spirit."

The two pitchers looked at me like I had done something wrong. I took off, and though I held my glove out to the outgoing pitcher, all he did was give me a grunt.

Coach Robert handed me the ball. "Don't give them a bigger lead."

I wanted to tell him that I could only do my thing. What batters did with the ball after I released it was up to them. But I didn't. In position on the mound, I gazed ahead at Ethan and threw five warm-up pitches that were generally on target. When the batter stepped up to the plate, it was a whole other ball game. Ethan called for a fastball down the middle. I nodded, liking the idea of sending a message. I placed two fingers across the seam of the ball and my thumb on the soft leather. When I released it, I watched it sail off course, drifting to the right. The batter recoiled from the plate. It was too late. The baseball hit him firmly on his shoulder. The crowd hissed, and I lowered my baseball hat and slinked back to the mound. I shook my head, ignoring the crowd and my own bench. One pitch, and a guy at first with a freebie.

Ethan approached the mound. "Way to fit in."

"That sucked."

"I'm only joking," he said. "Don't let it get to you."

"You ladies done chatting? Can we play ball?" the ump called.

With Ethan back behind the plate and a fresh batter up, I told myself that if I was never going to find Amanda, the least I could do for myself was to try and get a scholarship and some independence.

That awkward logic allowed me to get my next pitches on target, and I struck out the batter. Two more fly balls were caught, and then I was back on the bench.

The coach strolled by and gave me a pat on the head. I had to switch gears, from pitching to hitting. Unfortunately, the only advice I had ever received about batting was to not strike out. I tried to remember the batting cage, and how fun it had been to just let the bat fly. Ethan managed a line-drive single, and I stepped on deck. Three pitches later, I faced the righty. I let the first two pitches whiz past. One ball and one strike. Go down swinging, I told myself. The next pitch came at me low. I swung for the fences and missed. After that, I decided on the opposite strategy and used the batter's best friend—the bunt. The ball dug into the ground in front of the plate, and I sprinted to first, but the ball beat me there. Back at the bench, I was surprised when some of the guys gave me a quick round of applause for getting

Ethan to third. I only pitched one inning that game, but I was part of an inning that allowed us to tie the game.

After the post-game wrap-up, I was exhausted and told Ethan I'd talk to him the next day. I had a long walk home ahead of me and had worked the late shift the night before. About a thirty-minute walk in the opposite direction of the beach, just past a strip plaza where the rumble of the freeway was more present, I reached the small green bungalow where I was staying for the summer. There were bars in the window, and it looked run-down, but inside it was nicer and more welcoming. Most important, I had a place to sleep. I hit the pillow hard.

chapter eight

The end of my day shift was in sight. I cleared off the last tower of lunch plates. Luckily for me, Jessie had been working the front until about an hour before that. I tossed my apron in the laundry and headed out, exhausted but happy to see sunlight.

"Hey, Travis."

I turned to see Jessie sitting outside the Pineapple Hut. "You must be their number-one customer," I said. "You practically live here."

"What can I say? I walk in, they know my order, and I get to hang outside as long as I want. Where you heading?"

"Going to the library to do some research."

"You writing a paper?"

"Hell no. I'm going to do some online searching for Amanda."

"Well, I'm meeting some friends here. You're welcome to use my computer." She reached into her bag and pulled out a MacBook.

"You don't mind?"

"Of course not. Another reason I like this place is their free Wi-Fi."

I sat next to her as she logged in for me. I showed her my Facebook page. "You won't believe how many people set up Facebook pages to search for lost family."

I updated the title of my page, changing it from *Searching for Amanda* to *Searching for Amanda Miller*. "Thanks to you, I have a last name. I feel I'm one step closer." In the Facebook search bar, I typed *searching for* and slid the computer toward Jessie.

Jessie was blown away by how many people were looking for someone. "That's so crazy," she said.

"I set up my privacy settings so anyone can read it and friend me," I said. "I have about a thousand friends, but no leads. It's like people are using me just to get their friend count up!"

She flicked through some of the pages, and the necklace dangling over her T-shirt caught my eye. It was a silver medallion, and on it was what looked like a Greek guy holding a spear. Jessie looked up from the screen and caught me staring. "I wasn't..."

She touched the medallion. "It's St. Christopher. My dad got it for me when he was in Hawaii. It's the most cherished possession I have."

She knew a lot about me, and I hardly knew anything about her. I asked about her family, and she told me her parents had divorced when she was five. She spent most of her time flip-flopping between both homes. With a brother at Stanford, she said that her parents had high expectations of her.

55

Jessie stopped in midsentence. "I'm blabbing on about my family and you asked about my medallion."

"No, it's okay."

"One of the St. Christopher stories is that he was very strong and helped people get across a dangerous river. I'm a surfer, so that's why I wear it. It's like he protects me out there. It's a good-luck charm." She blushed. "And it makes my dad feel better. He hates that I surf."

"I guess everyone around here surfs."

"That's a stereotype. Oh, hold on—you're right!" She slapped my arm. "Have you ever surfed?" Without waiting for my reply, she said, "I tried baseball with you. You're going to have to try riding the waves with me."

"It'll be more like crashing the waves."

She laughed as two girls approached. Jessie gave me a quick introduction to her sister, Sophia, and her friend Mariah. They started talking and I tried a few new searches. I went to Google and typed *Amanda Miller Hermosa Beach California*. The search came back with a Molly Miller.

Sophia wrapped her long dark hair behind her ears and asked, "So, you're trying to find your sister?"

I nodded.

"And you know what?" Jessie held out the yearbook. "This is her."

The girls gathered around to check it out. My next search was through 411.com. It gave me a slew of names, but they were for Redondo Beach, Los Angeles and a few places I had never heard of, like Lawndale and Playa del Ray. After a few more searches, I still had nothing, so I closed the lid.

Mariah asked, "Wasn't what's-her-name in a book club with that girl?"

"What's-her-name?" Sophia repeated.

"You know. She moved here from Seattle." Mariah slapped her hand against her head as if that would help her remember.

"Christina?" Sophia asked.

Mariah shouted out, "That's her!"

"Let me see if I have her number." Sophia scrolled through her Blackberry. "Got it!" She turned away to make the call.

Jessie looked at me. "Doesn't hurt to ask anyone and everyone."

I didn't hold much hope.

Sophia hung up and turned back to us. "So, Christina has been out of touch with Amanda for a long time, but Christina's father worked with Amanda's father."

I couldn't believe she had actually found something that could help me. Finding Amanda's father could lead to finding Amanda. "Where did they work?"

"Some tech company..." Jessie, Mariah and I waited for what seemed like an hour for her to spit out the name. "Two Oceans Tech. Weird name, right?"

Jessie beat me to her computer and googled the name. At first glance, it looked like it was a company that designed navigation equipment for expensive-looking yachts.

"Click on the About Us section," I said.

Jessie opened a link, and a company directory appeared. The girls peered over our shoulders. Jessie scrolled down but didn't find anyone with the last name *Miller*.

"I don't get it," I said.

Sophia shrugged her shoulders. "Sorry, guys. I feel horrible. That's all Christina remembered."

I was disappointed, and I could tell Jessie was too. But what could I do? I thanked Sophia and Mariah. It wasn't their fault. I was getting used to dead ends.

chapter nine

The next evening, a day shift and two buses later, I joined the rest of the Hermosa Hurricanes in the outfield for our six o'clock game. I should've accepted Ethan's offer to drive me, but I felt as if that might be abusing the friendship—he'd been chauffeuring me everywhere. And, right or wrong, I knew Ethan's hanging with me put him at odds with the other pitchers. Out of breath and kneeling on one knee, I positioned myself in the second row with the rest of the bullpen, facing Coach Robert. Ethan was front and center.

The coach had already started his pre-game pep talk. "Hurricanes, we have a tough battle ahead of us. The Raiders haven't lost a game yet, and I'd like to make it so the buck stops with us."

Coach Robert shifted knees. "I want to remind everyone about the baseball weekend coming up."

Ethan turned around. I held up my glove, and he nodded. I listened to Coach Robert talk about the upcoming weekend tournament. He outlined the times. It sounded as if I was going to have to ask for the next weekend off work.

On my way to the bench, I paused so Ethan could catch up with me. "I had no idea about this tournament," I said.

"That's because you keep taking off. I know you're looking for your sister, but a lot of what goes on with the team happens before and after games."

I wasn't foolish enough to not know that the guys hung out and chatted online.

Being on a team was like being in a frater-
nity. Problem was, my life wasn't just playing
ball and surfing. I was a brother looking
for his sister. My part-time obsession with
baseball was getting me through washing
dishes. The summer my teammates were all
enjoying was a ticking time bomb for me.
At the end of August, I was out of here.
Sister or no sister. But what could I say to
Ethan? He was right.

"Two games ago, after you took off,
Coach Robert announced the weekend
tourney." Ethan shrugged. "I guess I forgot
to tell you."

He started to tell me about the tournament, but Theodore, the starting pitcher,
cut us off.

Theodore was the tallest guy on the
team. He had an incredible reach, which I
had been trying to copy. "Hey, E," he said.
"I got to start this game. You going to make
some time for me?"

I let them talk and took a seat on my
end of the bench. We were playing in a

different ball park tonight, but it felt the same as the last one. Maybe sitting in this spot wasn't so much a pitching order as it was a seniority order. Maybe I had to stop taking everything personally and just go with the flow. This was baseball, and I was the new guy. Maybe I should feel lucky that I hadn't had any hazing. Then again, maybe the pitchers' not talking to me was their form of working in the new guy.

The game started, and I quickly understood why the Raiders hadn't lost a game. Their starting pitcher had an incredible arm. He threw a curveball that dipped like a roller coaster. They got an early lead and kept adding insurance to it, a run an inning. Then, to my surprise, the Raiders' coach stepped onto the mound and pulled the pitcher. That was when the game changed. My guess was that he thought he'd given his team enough of a lead and there was no point burning out the pitcher's arm. Ethan started the seventh inning off with a double and was soon driven home. Changing the pitcher gave our batters a chance to make contact with the ball. At the third out, it was Raiders 6, Hurricanes 7.

Coach Robert offered some advice. "We're winning, but we haven't won. I pulled the starter, and he's icing his arm. Now I'm counting on you guys. Charlie, you're up. Mr. T and Davis, consider yourselves on deck."

I was disappointed not to be called up first. Charlie warmed up, and Davis looked at me.

"So you're from Arizona," he said.

I wondered if this was a trick question. "Yeah."

"Don't take anything personally. Especially from Charlie. It's just that we all want our game time. How else will the scouts see us?"

"That makes sense."

"We're on the same team, but we hope for each other to screw up," said Davis.

"I appreciate the heads-up." While I had Davis talking, I asked, "Why does the coach call me Mr. T?"

"He's only going to learn your name if he's sure you're going to stick around."

"Got it."

The crowd roared. A Raiders player had hit a double off the left-field wall. Then a bunt put a player on first and third. Charlie had no choice but to walk the next hitter to load up the bases and force a possible out at each base. Ethan and Coach Robert circled the mound.

Davis said, "You're lucky."

"Why?"

He pointed to Coach Robert, who was signaling me, and then to home plate. "Next batter up is a lefty."

On the mound, Coach Robert said to me, "Just do me one favor. All we need is one out, so don't walk him. If we lose, I want it to be square."

With Ethan's glove outstretched behind home plate and the Raiders hitter ready to go, I released a fastball as hard as I could. The hitter swung for the fences, but my ball beat him and punched into Ethan's glove. He made contact on my second pitch, but it drifted foul past third base. It was two and oh, and I was way ahead in the count. Ethan stood and approached me. I put my glove over my mouth and asked him if I had done anything wrong.

"No, I just want to stall. You're on fire against the best batter in the league."

"He's the best?"

"Okay. Shouldn't have said anything. I say we finish him off with another fastball."

I nodded. "Hey, guess what? I found out where Amanda's dad used to work."

"Can we *focus* here?"

"I'm standing in the middle of a stadium filled with a crowd that's hoping I mess this game up. Talking about Amanda helps to take my mind off that."

"Okay. Where does her dad work?"

"Well, the problem is, I don't think he works there anymore. It's a place called Two Oceans Tech."

"Yeah, they work on sailboat technology."

"You've heard of them?"

"Hey, look around. They sponsor our league!"

I spotted a banner with the company name on it. "You're kidding me."

"They're one of the biggest companies in Hermosa. Who do you think is helping to pay for our hotel for the baseball tournament?"

Behind us, the umpire called, "Do you want a delay-of-game penalty?" The crowd booed in support.

"Where's the tournament?" I asked.

"Riverside. About an hour away. Hey, I know a guy that works for Two Oceans Tech. He's the biggest baseball fan ever. I'll take you there on Monday, if you pitch a strike."

Fingers in position on the ball, I started my windup, said a quick and silent prayer and released it. The ball sliced through the air and caught the tip of the bat as it moved over the plate. The ball reached Ethan's glove on target, and I sighed in relief. The Hurricanes cleared the bench, and Raiders fans poured out of their stadium seats.

In the tangle of players, Charlie found me. "You got lucky, new guy."

I smiled and raised my arms. I wasn't going to let anyone ruin this moment.

chapter ten

Monday morning arrived, and I was up and out of the house early. I walked to the Hermosa Beach Pier. The morning sunrise was worthy of being computer wallpaper. The scene looked eerily similar to the postcard Amanda had sent. I reached the end of the pier and lost myself in the sun's glow. I had a good feeling that I'd find Amanda's adoptive father. A choppy wind pushed against my face, but I didn't mind. I wondered if my sister ever walked this pier and thought about me. What had motivated her to send me a blank post-card? I had more questions than answers. I had no way of proving the postcard was from her and that she even wanted me to track her down. I watched the waves break in a predictable pattern. By the time I turned to leave, I wasn't alone. Several people were fishing, their baited poles resting on the railing.

I watched a group of surfers wax their boards and head out into the surf as I waited for the restaurants and stores to open. I looked for Jessie but didn't spot her. No surprises there. Ethan texted me just after nine and picked me up at the base of the pier.

As he drove, he did a pitch-by-pitch breakdown of how great I had done the night before. The coach, according to Ethan, was looking forward to me pitching a lot more during the tourney. Ethan said I should be pumped because it was an event that college scouts attended. Then he threw a curveball at me. "So have you told Jessie how much you're into her?" he asked.

"What?"

"Come on. I know how much you like her. I can tell by the way you look at her."

I couldn't deny the obvious. "It's just a crush."

"So ask her to hang out one night after work."

"I can't. Without her, I wouldn't be this close to finding Amanda. I don't want to blow the friendship."

Ethan nodded as he pulled up in front of a modern, five-story glass building. "I'm just saying, if you like her, then make your move. The summer's short, and so is your time in southern Cal."

"I'll think about it." I followed Ethan inside. We took the elevator to the top floor, and a receptionist directed us to Mr. Perry's large corner office. A tanned man in pressed jeans and a white golf shirt reached out his hand. "Got to say I was surprised when I was told the great

Hermosa Hurricanes catcher wanted to see me. How're you doing?" he asked.

"Excellent. Thanks for seeing us without an appointment, Mr. Perry."

He directed us to two large chairs. "Call me Kevin, and I've always got time for my favorite team."

"This is Travis. He's new to the team," Ethan said.

Kevin shook my hand firmly. "Tell you, the only thing in life I didn't get was a son. God knows we tried. Four girls—can you believe it?"

I shook my head like I knew what he was talking about. Last time I looked, girls played baseball too.

"So what're your coordinates on the old diamond?" he asked.

I looked at him, trying to decode what he was asking.

"You know—your four-one-one?" he said.

Ethan stepped in for me. "He's an incredible pitcher. A southpaw."

"Fantastic. We haven't had a lefty since Rodriguez."

I nodded along with Ethan, trying to fit in. I scanned the office. There was baseball memorabilia everywhere, including a series of balls encased in glass.

He picked up one of the glass boxes and brought it to me. "I see you've spotted my gems. That one is from 2009. Probably just an ordinary night for you. But I was in the Bronx. It was game six of the World Series, and the Yankees were battling it out against the Philadelphia Phillies. Yankee stadium was alive. Next to my girls coming into the world, it was the greatest night of my life. The veteran left-hander Andy Pettitte was unstoppable. But the real pin-striped star was Hideki Matsui. He led the offense with a home run, double, single and six runs batted in. He was the first Japanese-born major-leaguer to win a Most Valuable Player award." He handed the baseball to me. "You're looking at his signature from that night."

I examined the ball. "You met him?"

"We didn't have coffee or anything, but several of us were introduced to him."

He placed the ball carefully back in its spot. "So, you guys pumped for the big baseball weekender?"

Ethan gave him an update on the season so far, including the details of our win against the Raiders.

When Kevin started tapping his fingers on his desk, I knew we'd eaten up as much of his valuable time as he was willing to give.

I sat up in my chair. "So, Ethan brought me here because I thought you might be able to help me."

"Uh-huh. Look, it's been awhile since I threw a pitch." He laughed at his own joke.

"Travis is looking for his sister, who he hasn't seen in a long time," said Ethan.

Kevin looked confused.

"Her name's Amanda Miller," I said.

"A Bob Miller used to work here," said Kevin.

"You know him?" I asked.

"Yeah, he had big dreams, quit his job. He started his own company about two months ago."

I wanted to stand up and jump out the large window. "Do you know where I might find him?" I asked.

"If I remember correctly, he left Hermosa for..." Kevin looked up at the ceiling, as if the answer was written there. "San Diego."

I looked at Ethan and thought about moving to San Diego.

"What about a new address?" Ethan asked.

"I can check. But it's not likely."

I stood. "Thank you for the help."

"Not a problem. Let me walk you boys out."

On the way to the elevator, Kevin joked that at least Bob hadn't moved to Australia. Then he turned the conversation back to baseball.

chapter eleven

My boss wasn't pleased that I had to go out of town for a family event. With each swipe over a dish, I racked my brain for ways to tackle San Diego. I knew no one there. And I needed another excuse to get some more days off.

After the lunch rush on Friday, I signed out and gave Jessie the San Diego update at the Pineapple Hut.

"That is such good news, Travis," said Jessie.

"It is, but it means I have to crack another city."

She reached for her computer and turned it on. "Well, that's what the Internet is for."

"If we go on 411.com, maybe her name will pop up when I exchange Hermosa for San Diego."

"Exactly," Jessie said.

I typed in *Robert Miller, San Diego* and got more than I bargained for. "There are thirty-five Bob or Robert Millers."

Jessie examined the screen. "Now you've got the opposite problem. But it's a good one. Just weed through them, and it'll lead you to Amanda."

"You're right. It's only thirty-five phone calls."

"And who's to say you won't get lucky on number five?" Jessie copied the list into a Word document and saved it to a USB drive. Within five minutes, she'd taken the drive into the restaurant and returned with a printout of the names and numbers.

Ethan pulled up to the curb in his Jeep. He tapped his horn, despite already having my attention.

Jessie followed me toward the Jeep. Ethan got out, took my backpack and tossed it inside.

"How's the all-star pitcher doing today?" he asked.

I smiled, embarrassed by his comment. Jessie gave me an extended hug as she wished me good luck. After a moment, Ethan cut in. "What about me?"

Jessie pulled back and rolled her eyes so that only I could see.

He persisted. "It's a big tournament, you know. There will be scouts there."

Jessie held her eyes on me. "You've got my cell. Call when you find her!"

"Thanks, Jess." I stepped into the Jeep, and Ethan hit the gas. With Jessie and the beach behind us, I patted the front pocket of my jeans, checking that the list was with me as we headed toward the freeway.

"So what was she talking about? She knows we're playing in a baseball tournament, right?" Ethan asked.

"Yeah." I couldn't blame him for being anything but 100 percent focused on baseball. I was about to switch topics when he did it for me.

"I saw the way she pulled you in for that big hug." He tapped me on the arm. "You asked her out. Obviously, it went well."

"No."

"No to what part?" he asked.

"To all of it."

He lifted his baseball hat and repositioned it. "Travis, I don't know how things work in Arizona, but on the west coast you have to make your move fast. A hot girl like that won't stay single for long. Hold on. Do you even know if she's single?"

"No idea."

"Has she talked about a guy? Mentioned anyone?"

"Nope."

"Have you seen her with a guy?"

I was growing tired of his line of questions. "No."

"That's sweet." He nudged me again. "Then the only possible guy is you—or me!"

"What about you, Ethan? I don't hear you talking about a girl."

"That's because I'm in between girls."

"Really?"

"Yeah, had to drop the last girl. She had major issues."

I turned from the road to him. "She didn't like baseball, huh?"

"Hated it!"

By the time we rolled into Riverside, the list was burning a hole in my pocket. The two-story motel we were staying in had a large banner at the parking-lot entrance welcoming all the teams. The lobby overflowed with ballplayers. Our room had two double beds and a TV.

Ethan tossed his bag onto the bed closest to the door. "We have a team dinner at a restaurant across the street."

I was hoping to be alone with my list. "I'm kind of tired—"

"You can't ditch a team dinner. Coach will never forgive you. We need to leave in ten."

Less than five minutes later, Ethan dragged me out the door. The restaurant was set up like an old-fashioned saloon. It was busy, and we found the Hurricanes seated at a long table in the back. Chips, salsa and pitchers of soft drinks already crowded the table. Other teams sat at tables next to us, and I think there was a competition to see who could be the loudest. I worked on my bottomless 7-Ups, and soon enough I had a legitimate excuse to go to the bathroom.

I picked a stall and started punching in numbers, using a long-distance calling card I had picked up when we had stopped for gas earlier. I dialed the first name on the list. An old man answered and didn't understand what I was asking. He called me Peter and seemed to think I was his grandson or something. Not the best start. I hung up.

81

On my next call, a woman answered and put me through to Bob immediately.

A man cleared his throat and said, "Bob speaking."

"I'm looking for Amanda Miller."

"Well, if you wanted an Amanda, why'd you ask for Bob?"

That was a good question.

"Whatcha selling?" he asked.

"Huh? I'm not—"

"Are you some sort of telemarketer?"

"I'm looking for Amanda. Does she live there?"

"First, I think you've got the wrong number. Second, it's dinnertime."

Before I could say sorry, he'd hung up. The next call rang forever before a woman answered. I decided to pose my question better. "Is Bob or Amanda there?" There was silence. "Hello?"

"I'm sorry. It's just that Bob passed away a few months ago."

"I'm very sorry for bothering you."

"Did you work with Bob?"

"No. I was actually hoping to find Amanda."

"Don't know an Amanda. Bob and I were married for forty-three years."

My finger was on the Cancel Call button as she went into a biography of his life, and I saw my long-distance minutes disappearing. Then the bathroom door swung open, and I heard people talking. I panicked, hung up on the woman in midsentence and flushed the toilet. When I got back to the table, the entire team broke into applause, hooting and hollering my name.

Ethan asked, "Did you fall in?"

I slouched in my chair, red-faced, and hid behind another glass of pop.

chapter twelve

I had to zigzag my way through the lobby in the morning just to get out. It was a sea of bobbing baseball hats. The blue team had taken over the lobby chairs, while the yellows hovered over computers in the business area. I felt bad for anyone who wasn't here for the tournament. I repeated the words *sorry*, *excuse me*, as my backpack, with my cleats, batting helmet, glove and the list of phone numbers, brushed against people. When I reached the exit, I had to lift my bag over my head just to squeeze out.

A honking horn caught my attention, and I jumped into Ethan's Jeep.

"If our first team is late because of this traffic, it counts as a no-show and we win by default," he said.

"That ever happen before?" My backpack rested on my lap. I wasn't going to let it out of my sight.

"Don't think so," said Ethan.

I spotted three baseball fields as we entered an already jammed parking lot. Ethan had to scramble for a spot on the grass. I trailed behind Ethan, who was almost jogging to the field.

Most of the people milling around were parents with coolers. A large sign had a list of all the teams. The Hurricanes-versus-Chargers game was scheduled for field two. Ethan led me on a narrow gravel path between two sets of stands, each facing out toward two fields. We popped out behind the home-plate fence and saw some members of our team already sitting in a dugout. I stepped inside.

Coach Robert checked us off his list. "Where were you guys, the gift shop?" he asked.

Ethan apologized for both of us. After the warm-up, Coach Robert called us in for the pregame pep talk. He gave his usual advice and reminded everyone that this was a single-elimination tournament. "We need to win in our pool today to move to the finals on Monday. So do your best. Make it count. Go down swinging, and remember..." He paused. "There could be scouts watching."

Thanks for the pressure, Coach! Between the rush to get to the game and the pep talk, I had built up a lot of nervous energy, and it sucked to waste it sitting on the bench. I was excited and anxious to play. But at the same time, I would have been happy if the Chargers had gotten stuck at the hotel and forfeited the game. Our team was fielding, so I moved to the far side of the dugout, where the players' bats were stored in little cubbies. I looked over to make sure Coach Robert was distracted by the game, then pulled out my cell phone and my list. I dialed the last number on the list, just to mix it up. The call went straight to voice mail. I knew that meant someone was home but on the phone. After the greeting, I left a message with my name, number and reason for calling. My next three calls, dialed randomly from the list, were dead ends. No one knew an Amanda.

I turned and spotted Charlie talking with Coach Robert. Davis was alone on the bench.

"What are you doing?" Davis said to me.

"Nothing."

"On the phone."

I nodded. It was pretty obvious.

"Who you calling?"

I didn't know what to say and was worried he might squeal to Charlie. I thought about lying. Then I remembered that other than Ethan, Davis was the only one on the team interested in talking with me for more than a minute. "I'm searching for my sister."

"She lost?"

I told him the story.

"Having any luck?" he asked.

I shook my head.

In the sixth inning, there was another three up and three down. Coach Robert called out my name, telling me to take over. Like a good soldier, I hit the mound, did my warm-up and steadied the ball for the first pitch. I had no idea if we were winning or losing. A quick glance at the scoreboard showed we were ahead by two. Ethan flicked two blocked fingers in my direction, calling for a split-finger fastball. I looked at the batter, his uniform bright orange. The pitch zipped under the bat. I caught the pass back, returned to the mound and hoped they'd all go that way so I could return to my list. Prepping for my second pitch, I noticed Charlie and Davis chatting. Was he telling him about Amanda? Charlie would probably find some way to use it against me. My next pitch was off target, and I was punished with a single. Stay focused, I told myself.

Ethan called for a curveball. Problem was, I had my eye on the lead off the runner on first was taking. I could get through this inning quicker if I picked him off. I broke from my stance and whipped the ball to first. He made it back to the first base. Ethan tossed me a look. Ready to deliver on that curveball, I saw the runner on first take an even bigger lead. I again whipped the ball to first and shrieked when it went wild, allowing the runner to advance to second base. Ethan made a visit to the mound, and I promised him I'd focus on the batter. I pushed the phone calls I needed to make out of my head and was able to get out of the inning undamaged.

Coach Robert pulled Ethan and me aside as we approached the dugout. "What was all that about? You two need to get on the same page."

We nodded.

As I grabbed my spot on the bench, my cell phone rang. I quickly hit Mute and turned to see the coach looking at me.

His hands were pressed against his hips. "Did I just hear that? Now, what's up with you, Mr. T?"

I could hear the murmur of someone talking at the other end of the line. "Sorry, Coach," I said.

"Do you have a sick aunt?"

"Excuse me?"

"Dog?"

"No dog, Coach."

"Cat? Fish? Catfish?"

I spun back with a quick no. I needed him off my back so that I could take the call. I angled the phone slightly away from my chest to let the person on the other end know I was still there.

"Then I'm trying to understand why you see the need for a cell phone in my dugout. Am I clear?"

"Yes." I looked toward Charlie, who didn't seem to know what was going on.

"Good." Coach Robert turned to Ethan. "Keep your pitchers in line. Davis, after this at bat, you're taking over from Mr. T."

I slipped to the far end of the bench and answered my phone call with a whispered "Hello."

A woman's voice said, "You're still there. You left a message on my machine. I want to let you know I don't know Amanda. Thought I owed you at least a call back. Good luck."

My stomach turned. I slouched my head and turned off the phone.

"Give me your phone," said Ethan.

"Leave me alone, please."

"Then give me that piece of paper you're always looking at."

He reached for it, and I pulled away. "I need this."

"We're playing an important game and you're goofing off."

I told him that trying to find Amanda was not wasting my time.

"Can you at least wait until after the game? There could be scouts out there."

"What's the difference? I'm pulled from the game." Ethan glared at me. "Fine," I said.

Two innings later, we managed to hold on to our lead and take the game. After handshakes with the Chargers, I walked with Ethan to the stands, where he introduced me to his parents. They were both tall, tanned and very put together. In other words, intimidating. His dad complimented me on my pitching, specifically my fastball. His mom asked me how things were going with my sister. I told her the lousy truth. Before they headed back to Hermosa, they said they'd be back on Monday if we made it to the finals.

Ethan and I hung back in the stands to watch the next game. "You got a problem with me making calls now?" I asked.

He smiled. "What do you think?"

I continued making calls until Ethan persuaded me to throw some pitches to keep my arm warmed up.

At the afternoon game, Coach Robert kept looking at me to see if I was on the phone. It was hard to resist, but I knew he was watching to see how committed I was and whether I was a player he could trust.

I wasn't called in until the last batter of the game, but I got the job done. The Hurricanes moved forward in the tournament. I was back in the coach's good books, and, more important, I could go back to making my calls.

chapter thirteen

On Sunday morning, Coach Robert arranged for an early wake-up call. I didn't like having to get up early, but it was nice being the only team in the lounge. There were no lineups for food. Coach reminded us all that if there's a tie, the team with the most points advances to the finals. Not only did we have to win both of today's games, but we also had to keep our runs allowed as close to zero as possible. That put all the pressure on the pitchers.

We arrived at the field early. The coach's plan was to rotate all the pitchers into the game. In the third inning the Bulldogs' bats came alive, and I was brought in to stop them. It was the first time I had been called in early in a game. They scored one run off a fastball I let rise too high, and I thought I had failed. But Coach Robert said he was proud of me for plugging the leak.

After the game, Coach Robert ordered us to stick together and told us to keep from getting distracted. We all went to the restroom, got drinks and sat in the stands to watch a team Coach Robert said would be in the finals. "Study them," he said. "Get to know your enemy." When I tried to sneak to the top of the stands to make another call, Coach Robert was all over me.

In game four, with a four-run lead for us, my biggest challenge was staying away from my phone. We needed to win this game against the Ravens to stay alive. With one out to go in the bottom of the seventh, we thought it was in the bag. Then Davis gave up a double and a single. He had no choice but to load the bases. Coach Robert paid Davis a visit, and I deflected a glance from Charlie. It was him or me. I knew Coach Robert was stalling to see who the Ravens were bringing out to hit. I'd get called if it was a left-handed hitter, and Charlie would take a right-handed hitter. The Ravens coach subbed in a hitter. I watched carefully as he exited the dugout, picked up a bat and took a practice swing. I was in.

The night sky had started to show. Davis reluctantly handed me the game ball and almost refused my high five. After my short warm-up, the batter stepped to the plate and took his position—batting right. He was a switch-hitter. I looked to the coach to see if he'd pull me out, but he didn't.

I gripped a fastball, predicting Ethan's call. After the last game, I'd promised to pitch whatever he wanted. Into my windup, I curled my right foot up and then extended it, bringing my arm with it. The ball left my hand at top speed, heading for the inside and high. The batter started to swing, then tried to stop himself, but his wrists broke.

The umpire yelled, "Strike!" and the Ravens bench reacted.

I held back a smile as I took off my cap, wiped the sweat from my forehead and placed my hat back on.

Ethan called for another strike, this one lower.

I released the ball, doing my best to push it low and out of the middle of the plate. As if in slow motion, I watched the ball dip and the batter swing. The ball dug into the dirt and bounced wildly in front of home plate.

Ethan dropped to his knees to block the ball, rescuing it after it rebounded off his chest blocker.

I let out a long breath, relieved to see the runner on third forced to retreat.

The umpire yelled out again, "Strike."

Ethan threw me the ball as the coach paid me a visit. Ethan joined us.

The coach looked at Ethan and then at me. "I've seen two up in the count and bases loaded end horribly before. In some ways, it's better to be behind—makes you hungry for the strike."

I nodded, unsure how this information was helping me.

"There are two types of batters," Coach said. "I'm hoping he's the kind who swings for the fences. Just keep doing what you're doing." He patted my back and walked away.

I asked Ethan what the second type of batter was.

He shrugged his shoulders and said, "Coach never gets that far."

"Okay." I kicked some dirt up with my shoe. "So you want a fastball, right?"

"I just want a strike. You want to go fastball up high and outside?"

"Or we could go fastball and inside. He won't be expecting it."

Ethan nodded. "And what if it trails across the plate? You heard the coach. He might swing for it."

"Then it comes down to speed. Bat versus ball."

"All right. Inside and high." Ethan returned to home plate.

I steadied my gaze on the strike zone and released my third fastball in a row.

The coach was right—the batter started his swing. He wanted the grand slam. My fastball was out of position and confused him. He had choked up on the bat, expecting it on the inside. Instead, it raced over the plate on the outside. He adjusted his swing at the last moment and missed.

Ethan jumped to his feet the moment the ball entered his glove and charged toward me. "Three pitches—that was awesome!"

People in the stands cheered and the Hurricanes applauded as Ethan directed me to the bench.

"If the scouts weren't watching you, they sure will be now!" said Ethan.

A crowd of high fives greeted me.

Coach Robert put his arm around me and turned to face the team. "We're moving on! Great job, Travis."

He had called me by my first name, and it wasn't obvious only to me. I saw the look on Charlie's face.

I was through more than half the numbers on my list, and still no Amanda. I wondered if I just had bad luck or if maybe her family's number wasn't listed. A burger in one hand, my phone in the other and the team out of earshot, I dialed yet another number. While it rang, I kept an eye on the Hurricanes, who were seated at a row of picnic tables. Next to the tables were four barbecues. Flipping burgers at one of them was Kevin Perry, the guy who used to work with Bob.

"Hello?" It took me a second to remember that my phone was pressed against my ear.

After eighteen phone calls, I had figured out how to get right to the point. "Hello, I was wondering if Amanda Miller lives there?"

I could hear that the woman on the line was typing. "Amanda Miller?"

"Yes. You know her!"

"No, I don't know an Amanda Miller. Can you hold a second?"

"Ah, sure." Her second turned into two minutes.

"I'm sorry about that. Just had another call come in. So is there anything else I can help you with?"

That was it. Going from sounding like she could help me to nothing. I wanted to yell at her. Instead, I hung up.

"Ready to take a break?"

I turned to see Ethan. "Huh?" I said.

"Will you be joining us for dinner?" he asked.

"Guess so."

"You should be stoked we won, and you're to blame!"

At the picnic tables, Kevin Perry asked how the burgers were.

Everyone responded with cheers.

He took off his apron. "You guys do not need encouragement, but I have to say, this team sure knows how to play ball."

The guys all shouted, "Go Hurricanes!"

"That's a big credit to you, Coach Robert. You're in the finals, and I never doubted you guys for a second!" Kevin shook hands with the coach. On his way out, he winked at me and said, "You got

Steven Barwin

some kind of natural talent, kid. You pitch like a Hurricane. See you tomorrow!"

Ethan was so excited about making the finals, I had to send him to Davis's room so I could make some calls. We had a team meeting and dinner scheduled in the evening. I would be surprised if I got through the rest of my list by then. I dialed another number, and a man answered. "Hello, Bob Miller here."

"Hi, I'm looking for Amanda Miller," I said.

"Who's calling?"

I stood up. "It's—" Click. "Hello?" Nothing. What had just happened? I punched the number again.

The phone rang, and the call immediately went to voice mail. "You've reached the Miller residence. Please leave your name and number, and we'll get back to you."

"Ahhh, I'm—" I hung up and burst into the hallway. I found Ethan talking to three players. "I think I found her!"

Ethan turned to me.

"She's in San Diego. Can you take me?"

The other players started to smirk, but I didn't care.

Ethan told them he would catch up with them later. "No way. You can't just leave. We're in the finals tomorrow."

"It's at like four in the afternoon. We'll be back."

"There's a meeting and dinner tonight. You're not going to San Diego."

I slid back into my room, and with my back pressed against the door, I dialed one more number. "It's me. I found Amanda. Can you pick me up?"

chapter fourteen

Jessie picked me up at the back of the motel, and then we hit the highway, heading south toward Temecula and on to San Diego. It was hard to believe that in two hours I'd be at Amanda's house. My mind raced through what I would say to her.

"Maybe you should have told the coach that you were leaving," said Jessie.

"He would have said no."

"I guess. But I don't get not telling Ethan."

"He would try to stop me. He doesn't want me to find my sister—he only wants to win tomorrow."

"That's not true. He cares about you."

That point was debatable, so I let it be.

Jessie overtook an eighteen-wheeler on the highway. "So the game plan is?"

"Meet her, reconnect, exchange information and rush back for the team dinner."

"You're going to want to spend time with her. You guys have a lot of years to catch up on."

"There will be loads of time for that. I'm going to finish this tournament for Ethan and then move to San Diego."

"You're leaving Hermosa? The Hurricanes?"

When I'd moved to Hermosa, I hadn't expected I'd meet anyone who would care if I stayed. "One thing at a time. Let me talk with Amanda first."

"And what about your job?"

I looked at her. "My what?"

"I'm just kidding."

"Hopefully, they can find someone talented enough to replace me!"

"I think if you stick it out, he might make you head dishwasher."

"Thanks."

She smiled.

The buildings of downtown San Diego gleamed in the distance. I played with the radio, changing stations. It was the only way to deal with my nervous energy. Between Jessie and me was the Google map I had printed out at the hotel. Jessie followed it, and eventually we rolled into a quiet neighborhood. I was lost. She took a palm-lined two-lane road to its dead end. My window was rolled down. I could smell the ocean. She turned again, and I took in the expensive-looking homes as we searched for number 1982.

Jessie stopped the car and pointed. "There it is. Second house from the corner."

The house was a white bungalow with light blue shutters, with a matching double garage. One tall palm stood at the base of some steps leading to two large wooden doors. As I stepped out of the car, my one thought was that Amanda had really landed on her feet. She'd been adopted by people with a lot of money.

"So what are you waiting for?" Jessie said as she moved toward the house.

I crossed the road and climbed the steps to the front door. Reaching toward the doorbell, I stopped. I had never been closer to finding my sister.

"You want me here?" Jessie asked.

I nodded, took a moment to fix my hair and get rid of my hat. I rang the bell and stepped back. After waiting patiently, I rang it again. "Don't tell me no one is home."

"But you spoke to someone on the phone."

"Yeah. It was a few hours ago though." Three more failed attempts, and we walked back to the sidewalk. After the buildup, this was a huge letdown. "Man, I can't believe this. Now what?" I said.

"You have a right to be frustrated, but we're going to have to come back."

"When I called, the man hung up on me. Maybe they're just not answering the door."

"Try calling again," Jessie suggested.

"No one's going to answer." I stepped toward the main window, but bushes were blocking it, so I walked to the side of the house.

"What are you doing?"

I passed an air-conditioning unit humming away. "I'm checking the back," I said and slipped into the backyard.

Jessie trailed behind me. "Travis, this is private property."

"I need to know if she's here." The backyard was sloped and looked over a scattering of homes. I could see a parking lot by the beach. I knocked repeatedly on a sliding glass door.

"This is trespassing. They could call the cops!" Jessie said.

"Jess, I don't have time for this. I need to know if my sister lives here." I pulled on the door handle. It was locked.

Jessie yanked my hand off it. "With a criminal record, you can say goodbye to any scholarship. Scouts won't touch you."

Her logic had no effect on me. "There's something going on here. That guy, Bob Miller—when I called and asked for Amanda, he hung up on me. I think Bob sensed who I was on the phone and is keeping Amanda from me."

"What're you talking about?"

"It makes sense."

"You're scaring me." Jessie started to walk away.

I banged on the back door. "Damn!"

She stopped at the edge of the house. "What time is your game tomorrow?"

"Late afternoon. Why?"

"Forget the team meeting, and forget the dinner. How about we come back later?"

I looked at her. My back and face were sweaty. "Okay."

We killed time and drove around the neighborhood. After burning through an hour of fuel, I tried the house again. No answer.

"It's late, Travis. We need to decide what to do," said Jessie.

"I need to stay, but you should go home. I can get a bus in the morning."

"I can't leave you. Plus, you wouldn't get back in time for your game."

"I'll be fine. This is more important."

"And what about Ethan?"

"He'll have to understand."

"You should at least call him."

I looked out the window.

Jessie snatched my phone and flipped it open.

"Give it back."

"Ethan's been calling you!"

"Jess, he's only calling to get me back to the tournament. He's set on winning. I'm set on finding Amanda."

She returned my phone. "I told you I'd help you find her, so that's what I'm going to do. This is your search, so we'll do it your way. What's your call?"

"Spend the night here. Go back to the house first thing in the morning."

"Okay, where are we sleeping?" she asked.

"You're looking at it. You can have the backseat if you want."

In a beachside parking lot that had a perfect view of the Pacific Ocean, we ate take-out burritos as surfers rode out the remaining minutes of shimmering sun.

"Wish I had my board. Those look like some toxic waves," said Jessie.

"It looks peaceful out there."

"Yeah. When I'm on my board, the world disappears. Especially when I hit a breaker."

I turned to her.

"It's hard to explain exactly," she continued. "It's sort of like I'm in another time—riding the last wave of the day, as it cuts in and out of the last bit of light, seems to last forever. You would like surfing."

We watched as the surfers retreated to a beach bonfire. In the darkness of the car, we settled in for the night. I tried to get comfortable in the passenger seat while Jessie sprawled along the backseat. My phone vibrated, and I held it up so Jessie could see Ethan's name on the caller ID. I let it go to voice mail. I started to dial the Millers' number.

Jessie shifted in the backseat. "It's late, and you're just going to scare them away."

I powered down my phone. "Goodnight."

chapter fifteen

I woke to the sound of a car door opening.

"Sorry. I was trying to be quiet," said Jessie.

It took me a second to figure out where I was. The bonfire was out, and the sun was rising. "We have to go," I said.

"It's not even seven on a Monday morning. I think we're okay."

But I rushed Jessie into the driver's seat, and we tore away from the beach, screeching to a stop in front of the house. I ran up and rang the front doorbell.

The door opened, and a man with a perfectly trimmed black beard with grey flecks in it appeared.

"Bob Miller?"

He studied me before replying. "We give to a local charity."

The door started to close, and I realized I looked like I had slept in a car. "No, Mr. Miller. I'm looking for Amanda. She lives here, right?"

He looked over my shoulder. I hadn't realized that Jessie was behind me.

She nudged me. "Tell him who you are."

"I'm Travis, Amanda's brother from Phoenix."

"Amanda doesn't live here. You've got the wrong house." He stepped back and closed the door.

I didn't know what to say. If Amanda didn't live here, where was she? I rang the bell a few more times before the door opened slightly and Bob told me to get off his property or he would call the police.

The door closed again, and this time I heard him bolt it.

Cops or no cops, I didn't want to leave. He clearly knew Amanda, and without his help, there was no way for me to find her. I yelled, asking for a number, address, anything, but he didn't respond. I felt Jessie's hand on my arm. She gently pulled me away from the door. I wanted to collapse on Bob's lawn and not move until he helped me. Let the police arrest me for trespassing and take me to jail. I didn't care. Maybe a judge would see everything I'd done to find Amanda and understand my situation. Maybe a judge could go right to family services, find my file, find Amanda's, and let her decide for herself if she wanted to reconnect.

Jessie snapped me back to reality when she asked me if I was going to be okay.

I hadn't realized we were back in her car. I shook my head.

"I understand if you're not okay. It makes sense to not be okay. I don't know what to say to you or how to help you right now."

"Mr. Miller could have helped, if he wanted to." I wanted to punch a hole through Jessie's car door. Instead, I pushed my head back against the headrest. "You heard how he said she doesn't live there. That was before he said we had the wrong house."

"I don't know."

"Trust me, Jess. I do. This is the right house."

Jessie rested her hands on the steering wheel. "I don't want to ask this, but now what?"

I shrugged.

"If Amanda lives somewhere else in San Diego, that means she has a life, friends, maybe a part-time job. I'll drive you down every weekend, and we can find her that way."

I looked back at the house and saw the garage door slide open. A shiny red Jetta pulled out, a surfboard on the roof rack. And it was definitely not Bob behind the wheel.

"Is that Amanda?" Jessie started the car.

"I told you Bob was lying." We pulled away from the house in pursuit of the Jetta.

"I have no idea what's going on," Jessie said. "And look how fast she's going. She definitely doesn't want us to catch up to her."

We struggled to follow each zig and zag Amanda made through the winding maze of neighborhood streets. With each jarring turn, my mind raced to find reasons why Amanda didn't want to see me. Didn't she miss me as much as I missed her?

"Dude, your sister can drive," said Jessie.

Amanda already had a lead on us when she gunned it through a yellow light and made a sharp left turn on the other side of the intersection. Horns honked, and my stomach dropped as Jessie hit the brakes, stopping just before the pedestrian line.

"Jess, I don't want to cause an accident. Maybe we should back off. She clearly wants nothing to do with me. Who am I to force her into seeing me?"

Jessie turned right and then swerved into a U-turn. "We didn't come all this way to not get any answers."

She was right. I deserved at least that. "You look out on the left side—I've got

117

the right," I said. We passed through two intersections, and there was no sign of her. Only ritzy-looking shops and restaurants. Then I spotted the Jetta with the surfboard, parked in a metered spot. "There she is. Pull into that spot."

Jessie cut the engine. "What's she doing in her car?"

"Probably making sure she lost us."

Jessie reached for her door handle. "Well, what are we waiting for?"

"If we go now, she'll drive off. I don't want to lose her again. Let's wait for her to make the next move."

"Good idea. I have to say—no offense to you—your sister seems kind of crazy."

"She was always the kind of kid that never backed down."

Jessie laughed. "My brother ignores me. He bumped into me on the beach with his friends the other day and walked right past me. It was as if I didn't exist."

"What's his problem?"

"I think I embarrass him."

The Jetta's door swung open. Amanda got out. Jessie and I followed her. She looked back, but we kept a safe distance away.

"Where do you think she's going?" Jessie asked.

"I don't know, but I'm getting a little tired of hiding from her." I knew I had to make my move. I just wasn't sure when or how.

"Yeah, I feel like we're doing something wrong—illegal."

"That's exactly how I feel." I slowed down when Amanda stopped to look in a store window. Go up to her, I told myself, and don't scare her. "Jess, hang back a bit. I'm going to go and talk to her." I moved around a row of parked cars so that I could get behind Amanda. I moved slowly. This was the moment I had been waiting for— our reunion. In the reflection in the store window, I saw her look at me. "Amanda, it's me. Travis."

She turned around and lowered her sunglasses. She wasn't Amanda.

chapter sixteen

She stepped toward me. "Why are you still following me?"

Confused, I put up my hands and backed away. "I'm sorry—I thought you were someone else."

"Just leave me alone."

She started to walk away, and I followed her. "But you came out of that house. Do you know Amanda?"

She wouldn't look at me.

I fired questions at her, hoping one would get a reaction. "Why did your dad not want to talk to me? I'm trying to find my sister. Do you know where she is? Is she in that house?"

Finally she paused. "I heard who you are, and my dad can't see me talking to you. I can't help you. I can't even talk to you."

Jessie stepped up beside me. "If you help Travis, answer some questions for him, we'll leave you alone."

"Trust me, I can't help you."

Jessie pressed her hands on her hips. "If you don't, we're going to find out everything about you. We'll start online, then we're going to move down here for the rest of the summer and follow you, talk to your friends, do whatever we have to do, even—"

She cut Jessie off. "Okay, okay."

Jessie nodded toward me. "Just answer some of his questions."

"You can save your questions," she said.

"Then just hear him out," said Jessie.

To my surprise, Jessie actually got the girl to listen. I told her the same thing I had told everyone else. I may have sounded like a charity case or a nut case, but I hoped to get my point across. I ended by explaining that we had thought she was Amanda.

"Here's all I can give you. My name's Claire. Amanda's my stepsister. You should know that Amanda used to talk about you all the time."

It felt good to hear that. Although it didn't matter, I asked, "In a good way or a bad way?"

"Both." Claire smirked. Her iPhone beeped, and she glanced at it. "Dad left Arizona and brought us to California so he could open his own business and all of us could have a fresh start. It wasn't exactly the easiest thing, moving. It was a rough change, for everybody. And as much as I detested my dad for it, I have made some great friends. I love San Diego. Amanda has let go of everything, including you. She's gone for the summer. I didn't get to say goodbye to her before she left because we were bickering about a guy I was dating. I haven't spoken to her lately. Travis, my dad's not a bad person. And right now, he's probably surprised more than anything. You represent Arizona and troubled times for his adopted daughter."

"I need to see Amanda," I said.

"I can't help you with that."

"But don't you think Amanda should be the one to decide if she wants to see me or not?"

Claire's iPhone beeped again. As she checked it, I thought for a split second about snatching it from her hands, knowing Amanda's number was probably in it.

"I'm late. I have to go. See that coffee shop across the street?" Claire said.

I nodded. The café was on the corner, behind a row of very tall palm trees. It had a purple canopy and a wraparound patio.

"Meet me in one hour over there," Claire said.

"You're going to speak to Amanda?"

She smiled. "See you in an hour. Oh yeah—please don't follow me." Then she walked away.

"Do you trust her?" Jessie asked.

"I have no choice."

"So what now?" she asked.

"We wait."

It was the kind of café that has a hostess. I asked for a table on the patio. Despite the scenic view, I kept my eyes on Claire's Jetta. I'd said I wouldn't follow her, but I wasn't going to let her slip away either. A waiter stopped by to distribute menus and take our drink order. He stopped by a few minutes later and seemed peeved when I told him we still hadn't decided.

Jessie's face was half covered by the large menu. "I don't think he's going to let us sit here for free."

"I'm really not in the mood for eating."

"That's a good thing. Have you seen the prices?"

I took a peek as the waiter circled around us like a shark.

"Two iced teas?" I asked.

"Sounds great," Jessie said.

"And what about something to eat?" the waiter asked.

Jessie pressed her elbows onto the table and looked up at the waiter. "You know, my friend is getting over a nasty stomach flu. So I think we're good with only drinks."

I could barely hold in my laughter as the waiter looked at me, pursed his lips and walked away.

"That should buy us some time," Jessie said. "If there's one thing I hate, it's a pushy waiter. If I acted like that, I'd never get tips." Jessie's cell rang.

While she was taking the call, our drinks arrived. I checked my watch. A small part of me dared to hope Claire would return with Amanda.

Jessie put her phone down on the table. "You're never going to believe who that was. Ethan."

"You gave him your number?"

"He's in San Diego."

"What?"

"And he's on his way over here."

"*What?*"

She cut me off before I could say anything more. "I couldn't lie to him."

"As long as he gets here before Claire," I said.

We were drinking iced-tea refills when we spotted Ethan speed-walking toward the café. He bypassed the hostess and stopped at our table.

"Who the hell abandons their team like that?" he asked.

I didn't have an answer for him.

"Sit," Jessie said.

Ethan ignored her. He was gunning for me. "I don't hear anything from you? You just disappear?"

He was making a scene, disrupting the other customers. "Ethan, I told you I needed to go to San Diego."

"And I told you it could wait."

"Well, obviously, it couldn't." I knew I shouldn't have skipped out on the team, but Ethan had no right to act like a jerk. "Why did you come all the way down here?"

"You're not answering your phone."

"So you track down Jessie to get to me?"

"It wasn't difficult. I called your work and found out Jessie had to cancel her shift at the last minute for a family emergency in San Diego."

"And my number?" Jessie asked.

"I called the restaurant on the way down and told them I was your San Diego cousin. By the way, your fake uncle's going to be okay." Ethan turned to me and demanded that I return to Riverside with him. When I said I wasn't ready, he told me I was throwing away my life for another one of my chance leads. He didn't understand that the baseball me wasn't the real me. Baseball was the reason I had lost my family in the first place. I wasn't going to let it do that again.

Jessie told Ethan to back off.

"Yeah, Ethan. You keep saying I'm throwing away my future. I've only been playing for a few weeks. Somehow I get the feeling it's your future you're trying to protect."

Ethan didn't respond.

"Are you my friend or the coach's watchdog? Because right now, it seems your only interest is in protecting your chance for a win–" I stopped. Claire had entered the patio. Her dad was behind her.

Claire's eyes were hidden behind large-rimmed sunglasses. "I'm sorry," she said. "I had to let my dad know. He would have found out anyway, and you're not the one who has to live with him."

Claire stepped aside, and Mr. Miller pulled up a chair. He cleared his throat, waved off the waiter and folded his hands on the table. "Amanda would like you to leave her and her family alone."

"If that's what she wants, I'll respect that. But I'm going to need to hear it directly from her," I said.

He looked at me, staring me down. Clearly, he wanted me to back off. But I had every right to want to speak to Amanda.

Claire bent over and whispered in her father's ear. He shook his head, and she stepped back.

"Mr. Miller, does Amanda know I'm in town?" I asked.

"Amanda's got a good life now, and I think you should be happy for her." He reached into his pocket, pulled out a check and placed it on the table in front of me.

Jessie, Ethan and I all saw that it was for a thousand dollars. "It's for you. Please—leave my family alone." He stood up and marched away. Claire followed him.

"I'm sorry, Travis. Now what are you going to do?" Jessie asked.

I picked up the check, took a breath, ripped it into pieces and watched them flutter to the table.

"Am I missing something?" Ethan asked.

I turned to Jess. "Did you see what Claire was wearing around her neck?"

She shook her head.

"A St. Christopher medallion!" I said.

"Really?" said Jessie.

Ethan shrugged. "I don't get it."

"If we push Claire a little more, she might cave." I jumped to my feet. "Beautiful July morning. What else is there to do? You said it yourself, Jess—these are some of the best waves you've seen."

"What are we waiting for?" she said.

"Hold on, guys." Ethan stood. "What's going on?"

"Sorry, Ethan," I said. "Surf's up!"

chapter seventeen

Hitting the beach in shorts, a T-shirt and
Converse shoes, I felt out of place among
the sunbathers and surfers. At least I wasn't
wearing socks. I took off my sand-filled
shoes. My feet sunk into the warm sand.
The beach was close to the Millers' house
and the spot where Jessie and I had spent
the night. Jessie and I searched the shore-
line for Claire, trying to pick her out of
a sea of faces. It was no easy task. Four
surfers with their boards tucked under their

arms approached. Three were guys, all with six-pack abs. The girl wore a bikini and was carrying a wetsuit.

As they passed, one of the guys asked, "What you looking at, dude?"

"Do you know a Claire Miller?" I asked.

I heard them laugh. Annoyed, I turned to Ethan and told him that since he knew what Claire looked like, he should feel free to help.

"You know, right now there's a team practice," he said.

"Right. You're only interested in making sure we get back to the game on time."

"Well," Jessie said, "at least we know where Ethan's priorities are."

"Just do this another time. I'll drive you back down here tomorrow."

"Tomorrow? Listen—forget it! I don't need your help. Just leave me alone," I said.

Jessie pulled me away from Ethan and suggested we split up to search the beach. She and Ethan would take the top half, and I would take the waterline. I walked toward the shore. The cool Pacific ran across my feet, and I scanned the sunbathers to my left and surfers to the right. Although I moved quickly, I saw almost fifty bikini-clad false-positives. A couple of surfer girls splashed out of the water. They looked at me like I was a creep. At the edge of the crowd, I decided I couldn't take it anymore. I waved Jessie and Ethan down.

I wiped sweat from my forehead. "Maybe we need to go back to the house and stalk her."

"You know, I was thinking, Claire lives near here but that doesn't mean she surfs here," said Jessie.

"How does that help us?" I asked.

"Check this out." She held up her phone. "Black's Beach has San Diego County's best waves. It says there's a submarine trench offshore that creates ocean swells with big peaks."

"So?" I asked.

"So there are offshore canyons, and the water goes from very deep to very shallow. This creates kamikaze waves," said Jessie.

"If you were surfing, would that interest you?" I asked.

"Hell yeah."

"Then let's roll!" I said.

Zipping north, we passed through a touristy beach town called La Jolla. Jessie said the people who lived there had a lot of money. I asked her if Ethan was still following in his Jeep behind us, and she nodded. Out of La Jolla and into the Torrey Pines area, some huge bluffs appeared on our left. The folks in this area had even more money. Before the Torrey Pines golf course, Jessie turned onto a small street. A packed parking lot was to our left. To our right, cars were parked on a dirt field. I spotted a sign on the grassless field that read *Black's Beach*. The Pacific loomed behind the bluffs ahead.

Jessie rolled down the windows and turned to me. "Told you this place was popular."

"All we need to do is find her Jetta, and we're in business," I said.

We drove slowly past Porsches, minivans and Chevy pickup trucks. People, no matter how much money they had, were here for the waves.

Jessie drove across the parking lot to a sandy road. A sign said *No drinking and no sleeping or camping overnight*. The car's wheels skidded as she turned left in the sand, and we entered another parking area. I caught a glimpse of the water and six palm trees next to two small buildings with solar panels. Along the rolling hills, I could now make out some homes. We reached a guardrail at the end of the lot, and Jessie looped around. Then I saw the Jetta, next to a black Honda Civic with a *University of California, San Diego* sticker.

"That's it, right?" Jessie asked.

"I don't remember the plate, but the color is bang on."

Jessie double-parked next to a Porta-Potty, and I jumped out. From the top of the bluff, the blue Pacific stretched out below us.

Ethan got out of his Jeep.

"How do we get down there?" I asked.

"No idea. We can check in that small building," said Jessie.

"Well, this looks like a dead end," Ethan said, taking a step back toward his Jeep.

I spotted a man approaching an suv, a wet surfboard under his arm, and asked him. He pointed and said, "There's only one way down from here, and it's thataway."

I thanked him, and we stepped over the guardrail. I looked down at a steep and rugged trail. "That looks like a five-hundred-foot drop," I said.

"Check out the sign," said Jessie.

It was a scuffed sign that read *Danger— Stairways and cliffs unstable due to rains. Do not use.*

"Well, there's no other way to go," I said. "At least there's a handrail."

I started down the path, zigzagging along the edge of the bluff. Halfway down, I got too confident and slipped.

"You okay?" Jessie asked.

"I'm fine, thanks," said Ethan.

"Ha-ha," she said.

When we all reached the bottom, Jessie stopped. "So how do you want to do this?"

"Well, Claire would be here to surf, not sunbathe. So let's walk the waterline and keep a lookout for anybody on the beach with a board," I said.

"For the record," Jessie said, "my respect for Claire as a surfer has just increased. I'm freaked out just looking at those heavies."

I nodded, and we set off down the beach. When I glanced out to the break, I was surprised by how many surfers were out there. "If she's not on the beach, I'm going to have to wait until every one of those surfers washes ashore."

Jessie said, "Then it's probably better to wait by her car. And you'll probably miss the game."

"Guys," Ethan said.

"Yes, I know my time's running out—"

"No." He pointed.

I turned around, and there was Claire. She was talking with some other surfers, her wetsuit unzipped and pulled down to her waist. I moved toward her, and she looked twice before recognizing me.

"You're kidding me, right?" She asked her friends to give her a minute.

"I just want one thing," I said, "and then I'll head off. You won't see me again."

"You shouldn't be here," she said.

I reached into my back pocket and unfolded the postcard of the Hermosa Beach Pier. I held it out. "Please give this to Amanda for me the next time you see her."

Claire looked at the postcard, then at me, but she didn't say anything.

I kept the postcard extended toward her.

Claire finally took it. She examined the picture, then flipped it over, revealing my crummy handwriting.

"What is this?" she asked.

"Amanda will know." I turned and headed back toward the stairway leading up the bluff.

"You okay?" Jessie asked.

I nodded and told Ethan I was ready to return to the tournament.

chapter eighteen

In the Jeep, Ethan didn't say anything for almost the entire drive back to the tournament. I knew he thought going to San Diego was a waste of time, and he probably hated Jessie for taking me there. He had to race to get us back for the four o'clock game. We needed to be there by the start of the game, or we wouldn't be eligible to play. He had brought my uniform and glove with him. I changed as he drove, and he changed at red lights. When we screeched into the parking lot, our team was already on the field. I sprinted behind Ethan, noticing that the stands were full. As we got to the dugout entrance, I saw our starting pitcher finishing his warm-up. Coach Robert uncrossed his arms and pointed his index finger at Ethan.

"Not even one minute to go."

"Sorry, Coach," said Ethan.

Coach Robert looked away for a moment, as if he had a decision to make. "Get out there."

I started to follow Ethan, but the coach stopped me.

"Do you understand that I should kick you off the team for leaving the ball park and hanging your team out to dry?"

I knew better than to speak. I nodded.

Ethan surprised me by stepping forward, but the coach shooed him away and took a deep breath. "I've got a tournament to win, so sit down."

I took my usual spot on the bench and realized that Charlie and Davis had heard everything.

As the game started, Davis said, "Everyone's been wondering if you were coming back. Where were you?"

Charlie cut him off. "Why you talking to that guy?"

"Just a question," said Davis.

When Davis asked if I was still on the team, I told him I wasn't sure, and Charlie smiled. College scholarships were on the line, and scouts were everywhere. I didn't blame him for being competitive.

Five and a half innings in, the Hammerheads were up by two. I was wearing a jersey, but I didn't know if the coach was going to play me. I felt empty, knowing that my fate with Amanda was out of my control and in the hands of Claire. I had done all I could for now. I just hoped I had penetrated her overprotective family.

The roar from our bench pulled me out of my fog. A Hurricanes player had crossed home plate. By the bottom of the sixth, the game was tied. Our last batter went down swinging, and the Hurricanes bench emptied. Coach Robert stayed with his starting pitcher for the final inning. Davis and Charlie were itching to get in the game, while I just wanted to know if I was still on the team. I reached into my backpack tucked under the bench and snuck a peek at my phone. There were no calls from Claire or Amanda.

The distinct crack of the bat filled the diamond, and the Hammerheads batter took his position on first base. Ethan visited the mound for a quick chat as the go-ahead run stepped to the plate. The first pitch went high, and the runner on first stole second base. The second pitch hung over the middle, and the batter sent the baseball flying deep into right field. As the runner on second rounded third, the throw came in. It was enough to force the hitter back to first, but the runner on second scored, and we were now down by one.

Coach Robert jogged to the mound, and I stood up with Charlie and Davis. One of us would be picked. After an exchange with Ethan and the pitcher, Coach Robert turned and tapped on his left arm.

Charlie slung his hat over his eyes, and Davis called out, "I'm here if you need me!"

Stepping onto the plush green grass, I scanned the stands. At least Amanda knows I'm alive and that I'm reaching out to her, I thought.

On the mound, Coach Robert handed me the baseball and said, "Keep the ball away from the bat."

I smirked. Best advice I ever got.

Ethan returned to his position.

I took my first warm-up pitch and imagined Amanda receiving the postcard. I could hear Amanda saying, *What's this? I didn't send it.* My last pitch slid off my fingers, and I closed my eyes as I saw Amanda ripping up the postcard and tossing it.

The batter touched the tip of his bat with the plate and laid his gaze on me. The smack of leather on leather was what I needed to clear my mind of everything except the sport I'd come to love again. I checked the runner on first and delivered two more strikes. One down, two to go.

The next batter made the amateur mistake of swinging for the fences on everything I sent his way. He was "going for the glawr-ee," as my old coach used to say. I sent him packing. He'd have to wait for another opportunity to get his fifteen minutes of fame.

Runner on first, I told myself. Two out. You can do this.

The next batter approached. On the top of my arc, I flinched when the runner on first took off. The pitch landed high, and I hit the ground as Ethan sent it whipping over me. When the dust cleared, the runner was smiling proudly on second base. Things had just gone from difficult to DEFCON 1. The second baseman handed me the ball, and Ethan stepped away from the plate with his glove extended. He wanted me to walk the batter to force a possible out at third. But with more men on base, we could fall even further behind.

Ethan shook his glove like he was waving at me, but I didn't throw the ball. When the umpire shrugged, Ethan approached me. "What's your problem?"

"I'm not putting another possible run into play."

"It's an aggressive play and the right thing to do."

"Too gutsy. Ethan, I can get him out."

The crowd started to chatter, but I didn't care.

"This is how we do it on the Hurricanes."

Coach Robert approached the mound and interrupted us. "Guys, what's the holdup?"

"Just trying to walk him so I can set up the forced play if there's a grounder, Coach," said Ethan.

The coach looked at Ethan and then at me. "Walk 'im."

Coach Robert disappeared, and Ethan smiled.

"What's your problem?" I asked. "What did I ever do to you other than make you late to a ball game?"

Ethan didn't respond.

"You didn't get that I was trying to find my sister. And I think that was just a little bit more important than this."

"Easy for you to say."

"Huh? What does that mean?"

"Nothing," Ethan said.

"I'm not walking that batter until you tell me—"

He jumped in. "I brought you to my team, and what does the coach do? He makes it my job to watch over you. Don't you get that if you hadn't shown up today, I'd be off the team?"

"I don't understand."

"He knows you've got the potential to go all the way. It's every coach's dream to send a player to the majors. You win, he wins."

"You should have told me. I don't know why the coach made you do that."

"It means I'm replaceable. The coach was going to wait until after the game to tell you—"

The umpire caught us off guard. "Throw that ball, or it's a delay-of-game penalty!"

"Sorry, ump," Ethan said.

"Tell me what?"

"Walk him, get the next guy out, and I'll tell you."

I walked the batter. With runners on first and second, I faced a menacing-looking right-hander. My first pitch was fouled deep into left field. That was too close for comfort. I delivered a ball just to see how hungry this Hammerhead was. Unfortunately for me, he didn't bite. My next pitch swerved inside. He swung and missed. Ahead in the count, I started to breathe again.

Before I could celebrate, my fourth pitch drifted just outside the batter's box. This guy was good. Anyone else couldn't have resisted the temptation to swing at it. Two and two, and I didn't want to get into one of those full-count scenarios. I'd seen too many baseball movies and didn't have the stomach for it. Ethan called for a strike. It was dangerous. This batter could easily turn my speedball around and catapult it.

I wound up and tried to drill the ball down and inside toward Ethan's target.

The batter swung and drove it as low as I had thrown it. The ball bounced once in front of the mound and came at me chest-high, like a bullet. On pure instinct, I pulled my glove and squeezed. I stayed on my feet but was turned around by the force. When I looked in my glove, I was surprised to see the ball there. The runner on second was headed to third. I fastballed it in time for the third baseman to tag him out. Somehow, I had pulled us out of the inning alive.

Ethan fist-pumped me.

"I'm sorry, Ethan."

"Told you you'd need the forced play."

"I'm sorry for wasting your time and dragging you to San Diego. I should have respected you and the team."

"Don't worry about it. I told you—starting tomorrow, I'm happy to drive you wherever you want."

I nodded.

"So, you planning on going to university?"

"Yeah. Why?"

Ethan smiled. "Coach said a scout's interested in you."

"Really? From where?"

"University of California, Irvine."

"What? Really?"

"Yeah."

"Coach and the scout are hoping you spend your last year of high school right here."

"But I live in Phoenix."

Ethan laughed. "You couldn't ask for a bigger opportunity. I think your family will understand. Now promise me you'll act surprised when the coach tells you."

"I will."

"And no celebrating—yet. We're down by one, up to bat. You're lucky I took you to the batting cages, because you're up after me."

At the bench, Coach Robert pulled me aside and told me he had been waiting for my pitching duties to be over to share his good news. I kept my promise to Ethan.

chapter nineteen

I heard the crack of a bat and some applause from the crowd as I rummaged through the collection of bats in the dugout and grabbed one. With one out and a runner on first, all the pressure would be on me unless Ethan homered. "Promise me you'll get a home run so I won't have to bat," I said.

Ethan smiled. "You'll be fine."

"I think I forgot how to hit a ball."

"Every pitcher expects a pitcher to bunt."

"So?"

"So don't bunt!" Ethan pointed to home plate, and I took his place on deck. "I gotta go."

"We're good, right?"

"Yeah, we're good. Brothers from different mothers."

I laughed and fired off a round of practice swings on deck. Then I positioned myself as if I was up at bat. When the Hammerheads pitcher threw his first ball, I swung.

Ethan swung at the next pitch and made contact. The ball rocketed over the second baseman and deep into the outfield, where the center fielder chased it down at the wall. Thank you, Ethan, was all I could think, and then the ball dipped down and rebounded off the wall and into play. Ethan was forced to hold up at third, but he had got a run in. The game was tied, and the spotlight turned on me as he became the go-ahead, game-winning run.

I was hoping the Hammerheads would walk me, but stepping into the batter's box, I quickly found out that they didn't want to waste an easy out. The first pitch came inside and fast, forcing me away from the plate.

The umpire called a strike.

I adjusted my helmet and ran through my options. Despite the warning pitch to back off, I could crowd the plate, hope to get hit and take a bruiser for the team. That would be an easy way onto base.

Back at the mound, the pitcher did a good job of covering up his grip. Don't go down looking, I told myself, go down swinging. The next pitch whipped toward me, and I only had a blurred look at its approach. I started my swing and then tried to adjust it as the ball swerved right. Pushing right through it, arms extended, I heard the echo of the ball in the catcher's mitt.

"Strike two!"

I looked back to confirm I had missed the ball. I exchanged a look with Ethan. He pointed to his right knee and lifted it off the ground. Then he planted it firmly down and gave me a thumbs-up. It took me a second, but I figured out he was telling

me not to raise my foot off the ground
when I swung.

With me in the batter's box and down
two in the count, the Hammerheads
pitcher must have known he owned the
situation. I was only a hiccup on his way to
getting his team into extra innings. I figured
he wouldn't waste a ball on me when he
could get me down in three. He started his
windup, and I pushed the heels of my feet
into the soft dirt. Not wanting to swing for
the fences, I started my back rotation early.
Eyeballing the location and speed of the
ball, I simply wanted to get my bat on it.
The pitch started a right-to-left movement.
I only knew one thing—every batter's got a
weak spot. It was my job to find my own.
It must've been on the inside, because that
was where he was heading again.

The pitch zipped in front of the plate,
and I sped up my rotation—back to front.
Feet firmly down, my elbows brought my
hands in and I pushed the bat across the
plate to where the ball was. Expecting to
hear a loud crack, I heard what sounded

more like a thud. I'd made contact, but it took me a moment to find out where I'd sent the ball. It arched lazily into the air and drooped well behind the first baseman.

I heard the coach shout, "Run!" and I dropped the bat and took off. On my way to first, I spotted Claire. I did a quick check over my left shoulder and saw Ethan cross home plate as the go-ahead, game-winning run. The Hurricanes started to pour out of the dugout. I approached first base at top speed and saw a girl who was definitely Amanda standing next to Claire. I hit the base and blew past it, veering off the field toward her. I stopped at the chain-link fence separating us. It took them a second to realize it was me. I jumped the fence and pulled off my helmet. Amanda stepped forward.

She looked different, yet her eyes were the same. There was a long, uncomfortable silence.

Claire broke it. "Awkward."

I had spent all this time looking for her, and now I didn't know what to say.

"So how are you?" Amanda asked. "That's a stupid question, right?"

"No. I'm okay."

She let out a short, nervous laugh. "I can't believe you're standing in front of me."

She hugged me as loud cheers exploded like fireworks behind us.

"So you got the postcard. You were always the only one who could read my handwriting," I said.

"Yeah, I had no idea what it said!" Claire smiled.

"I always felt bad that we never had the chance to say goodbye," said Amanda. "Everybody told me not to call you. The postcard was my way of letting you know I had moved, and that I was doing okay. It took me two years to finally send it because I kept coming up with reasons not to bother you. "

"It's been tough. When I saw the post-card, I knew it was from you."

"We shouldn't have let them split us up. We should have tried to stay together. Looking back, it's easy to—" Amanda stopped.

"I'm glad you found me. I hear you were persistent."

"Oh, yeah," Claire said. "He was a total pain."

Amanda laughed.

"So where were you?" I asked.

"Visiting a friend in Los Angeles," said Amanda.

"And is your dad okay with you being here?" I asked.

"Probably not. I bounced around in the system before the Millers adopted me. When you showed up at our house, Dad... Bob...was worried that you were there to take me away. My adoptive parents have always been worried about that."

I nodded.

"But eventually they'll see that my having a relationship with you isn't their decision." She paused. "Were you adopted?"

"No."

"So you're living in the same foster home?" Amanda paused again, realizing that the answer to her question was obvious.

"Who's your girlfriend?" Claire asked.

"Jessie's a friend. Someone I met out here who helped me find Amanda."

"There he is!" someone shouted.

I turned around to see Ethan and Davis.

"This her?" Ethan asked.

"Yes," I said.

"Congrats!" He turned to Amanda. "I can totally tell you're brother and sister. Do you mind if we borrow him? We'll have him back in five minutes." Ethan and Davis propped me up on their shoulders and led me to the third-base line, where the Hurricanes were still celebrating.

chapter twenty

After I found Amanda, the stress in my life disappeared. All of a sudden, I wasn't washing dishes to support my search for her. I was doing it because it gave me money to save toward my future. On my breaks with Jessie, we talked about all sorts of things—normal things. It was as if the clouds had opened up to clear skies, and my relationship with Jessie grew and changed. It felt great to hold her hand.

"Did you speak to your foster parents yet?" Jessie asked.

"This morning. They want the best for me. I'm starting to realize how lucky I've been to have them. Their friends said I can stay on with them in Hermosa for my last year of high school."

She took her eyes off the door and faced me. "That's awesome! I'm so excited! It's going to be a great year."

"I'm more anxious about that surfing lesson."

"Stop it! You'll be fine." Jessie stepped closer to me, our hands still together. "I'm so happy you don't have to leave."

I leaned in for a kiss but was interrupted.

Ethan high-fived me and rolled it into a short hug. "So, Jessie, we going to show this boy the real Cali?"

"You bet." She laughed. "Soon he'll be wearing flip-flops and checking the surf report."

Ethan moved toward his Jeep. "So, we ready for this?"

I looked at them both. "I think it's time."

Redondo Beach appeared and then disappeared as I bobbed up and down in the midday sun. My hands gripped the surfboard as the cold water attacked my legs. I could barely feel them anymore. I wished I was in a head-to-toe wetsuit. "How come I'm the only one who can't do this?" I looked to my left, trying not to tip myself over. Jessie, Ethan, Claire and Amanda were all on surfboards.

"You can do this," Amanda said.

"Did you see my last two wipeouts? And I wasn't even standing!"

She tried not to laugh. Everyone tried not to laugh.

"The problem," Amanda said from her board, "is that they are all pros. I'm far from perfect, and not nearly as good as them. So try it my way."

I released one hand from the board and used it to paddle closer to her.

"Ready?" she asked.

"Okay," I said.

"I'm just going to tell you what I do when I surf. So lie flat on the board again."

I got down on my stomach like her.

"His hands are gonna make him tip," Ethan said.

Claire, Jessie and Amanda shot him a look.

He shrugged. "Sorry. Only trying to help."

Amanda continued. "Take your hands off the rails of the board and put them under your chest, flat on the board so your thumbs touch."

"Because it's more stable," Ethan said, proving his point.

"Now"—Amanda demonstrated—"do a push-up."

I pushed up with my arms and legs and found myself in an uncomfortable position, like a dog trying to surf.

"Now jump up!" she said.

I propped myself up awkwardly, nearly tipping the board. "I'm up. Now what?"

"Well," Amanda said, "you've got to do this closer to the takeoff zone. You know—where the waves are."

Ethan appeared behind my board and started to push me. "Don't worry about it. I have you covered. You should be doing this into the wave, but it's good enough for now."

My goal was not to fall.

"Catch the wave when you feel it moving under you. Hit it too early, and you'll miss it. But hit it too late, and you'll wipe out," said Amanda.

I looked over at her. "Thanks."

"No problem. Okay, here comes a wave," she said.

I kept my hands out like I was on a tightwire.

Ethan gave me a big push, and I glanced back to see white water rolling toward me.

The girls shouted out that I could do it.

Ethan offered one last word of wisdom. "It's like being at bat. Bend your legs!"

Getting down lower on the board seemed to help. The water rushed around me, and somehow I was still standing. I was doing the impossible. I stayed balanced and, with the girls applauding and hollering behind me, I rode my wave toward the beach.

Author's Note

When I came up with the initial idea for this book, I spoke with staff at lots of foster-care agencies in California and was surprised to find that, despite agency policy or a case worker's best efforts, siblings are often permanently separated. Then my idea started to morph, and I wondered how frustrating it would be to be separated from my sister and have no way of reconnecting with her, constantly feeling like a piece of me was missing.

Baseball was the perfect vehicle for the story, and California was the perfect venue. It's one of my favorite places in the world and is known as the baseball factory of the United States, producing many talented players. As much as I like baseball and enjoy playing it, my real knowledge about baseball comes from conversations with my grandmother, who was a real expert. The Blue Jays were her team of choice, and we shared many in-depth conversations about the sport over the years. By combining her passion for baseball and mine for the mystery genre, I think I've got a book that my grandmother would be proud of!

Acknowledgments

My first big thank-you goes to Leslie Bootle at Orca. We met at the Ontario Library Super Conference, and without her, *Hurricane Heat* never would have happened. Thanks for the vote of confidence! Thank you to my editor, Christi Howes, whose encouragement, insightful comments and incredible eye for detail were invaluable. Thank you to Sarah Harvey for adding finishing touches and seeing my book to production, and to my agent, Lynn Bennett, whose guidance, encouragement and enthusiasm for this novel helped motivate me.

This book would not have been possible without research. I wish to thank the USA Premier Baseball League for its help with the nitty-gritty ins and outs of the league.

To the Los Angeles County Department of Children and Family Services, the National Foster Parent Association and the Alliance for Children's Rights, thank you for your patience as I bombarded you with countless questions. I have newfound appreciation for the incredible work you do each and every day. Finally, I wish to thank my family for their love and support and for allowing me to follow my passion and write every day.